CASSIE MINT

Blood, Sweat & Kisses
The Complete Series

BLACK CHERRY
PUBLISHING

Contents

I

Fight Dirty

Description

H e's brutal and battered. **The meanest fighter in the city.**

And I'm begging him to teach me how to fight.

The first time I step foot in Jax Sutherland's gym, he stares like I'm some badly lost tourist. All around, men are beating each other to a pulp, and I wince with every smack and grunt.

Maybe I *am* lost. Coming here is definitely the craziest thing I've ever done, and I'm so out of place it hurts. I'm a cuddler, not a fighter, and I can't even watch scary movies. This is nuts.

But I'm desperate. Someone's been following me through the city, leaving threatening notes, and I'm so tired of feeling afraid. Feeling vulnerable.

I need to learn to defend myself, and for that I need Jax.

At first, he laughs. Then he scowls.

Then he drags my flushed body to the mat.

Casey

~~~~~~~

I dither on the sidewalk, my clammy palms tucked into my hoodie sleeves. It's evening, the sky pink above the city rooftops, and all around traffic rumbles and feet thud against the sidewalk.

Lights change and horns blare. It's my favorite time of day. Tonight, though, I'm too wired to enjoy it.

I'm downtown, where the delicious scents of curries and roasting meat mingle in the air and crowd out the traffic fumes and cigarette smoke. My stomach growls under my baggy layers, nudging me to go somewhere else, *anywhere* else on this block so long as they serve something spicy and sweet. Any of these restaurants with their steamed over windows will do.

But I ignore it. I'm a girl on a mission.

Tonight, I'm going to find Jax Sutherland, and I'm going to talk to the famous fighter, and I'm going to persuade him to teach my reedy ass how to fight.

I *am*, damn it.

Shifting from foot to foot, I stare up at The Corner. I wet my lips. The lights are bright inside, all the doors and windows thrown open, and the grunts and thumps of fights float out to the sidewalk. I hide a wince.

The sign above me is black and white, all business and no frills. Men and women pass by in a steady stream, entering the boxing gym with neat workout clothes and staid expressions, while the folks coming the other way are flushed, sweaty and rumpled. They all look like they've been electrified.

That doesn't seem so bad. Right? I like an adrenaline rush as much as the next girl. At the fairground, I'm always the first one making a beeline for the roller coaster, and I'm...

I'm stalling again.

Come on, Casey. Get your ass in there.

As I fidget before the doorway, the scraps of paper crinkle in my hoodie pocket. They may be lighter than a fistful of feathers, but every time I notice them, it's like they're weighing me down to the bedrock beneath the city.

They're the reason I'm here. The reason I can't fail tonight.

I *need* to speak to Jax Sutherland, and it's that reminder that finally gets my feet stumbling forward, my shoulder brushing the door frame as I enter.

The Corner is even bigger and brighter and louder than it seemed from the street, the walls painted white and lights dangling in wire cages overhead. It's a few degrees warmer than outside. Music thumps from speakers clustered on the walls, a steady beat without any lyrics, and all around pairs of people square off, swinging fists and ducking, weaving, kicking.

There's a boxing ring in the center of the huge room, and punching bags hang from thick chains all around the walls. Mats are piled high near the door, and a few pairs have dragged mats down to the floor so they can grapple, rolling together in a vicious tangle.

"Holy shit," I mumble, drifting forward in a daze. Despite my time spent lurking on the sidewalk outside, I am not prepared.

It's just so *big* and loud and overwhelming. When a flushed man with a shiny bruised eye looks my way, I flinch, skirting around the edge of his mat. He looks like he could pick his teeth with my bones—and mean enough to do it, too.

Focus, Casey.

Jax Sutherland. Jax Sutherland. How the hell am I gonna find him in here? This boxing gym is like a cavern hidden downtown in the city, the ceilings soaring high overhead and the open room sprawling wide. There must be dozens of pairs fighting here, spread out so much that they're lost in their own private worlds.

Fingers trembling, I fish my phone from my pocket, walking slowly through the maze of mats and sparring fighters. The photo of Jax Sutherland is already loaded on my screen—and I frown down at it like I haven't stared at him for hours already. Like I haven't committed his scowling hazel eyes and broken nose to memory. Like I'm totally, one hundred percent normal about this complete stranger.

Nope. I check each man I pass, glancing down at the photo now and then. No. Nuh-uh. Hair too light. Too wiry. Too young.

This is Jax's gym, and god knows I could probably just ask someone if he's here, but I'm too much of a weenie to engage any of these brutal fighters. So I wander through the labyrinth, flinching at every loud grunt and smack, and by the time I reach the boxing ring, I'm sweating like I've had a workout too. My stomach's still squirming, but now it's pure nerves.

Two men square off in the ring, both bare-chested with black sweatpants hanging low on their hips. Both are tattooed; both slick with sweat, bare arms shining in the bright light. They both look like they could squish me like a bug.

But only one makes my cheeks flush bright pink.

Jax.

I check my phone again to make doubly sure, my hand so shaky I nearly fumble and drop it.

Yep. That's Jax Sutherland. The man pummeling his opponent, forcing him back into a corner; the man with a hard jaw and a fierce glint in his eyes. He's an inch shorter than the other man, but he makes up for it with broad shoulders and that calm, relentless attack—the one that earned him the nickname 'The Terminator'.

No displays of emotion. No gloating or whining. In his day, Jax Sutherland took down opponent after opponent with merciless precision, and watching clips of his fights in my bed last night… well, it made my tummy swoop. And it's weird, but seeing him *now*, a little older and somehow even calmer…

I shove my phone back into my pocket, and I will *not* fan myself. I will be normal about this.

The fight is short, and part way through, Jax Sutherland's hazel eyes drift over to me—and stay fixed. Sparks skitter under my skin, and I flush even warmer. God, why didn't I put on makeup to come here? Why did I wear my slobbiest, baggiest workout clothes? I look like I rolled around in a pile of laundry and came here in whatever stuck to my limbs.

Maybe that's why Jax is staring. But he takes a blow for that moment of distraction, his head snapping back, and then he looks away. The fight gets faster. Meaner. Flecks of sweat fly out of the ring, pattering against the floor, and I bite my lip, my whole body tense.

The music throbs. Punches smack into skin. Grunts float from all around, and I'm dizzy with how out of place I am here. I *hate* violence—I'm twenty one years old and I still think carefully about any movie that's over a PG rating, for god's sake—and if anyone so much as brushes past me, I might burst into tears.

But I'm here. I've come all this way, and I've found Jax Sutherland.

The papers crinkle in my hoodie pocket, and I blow out a deep breath.

I'm doing this.

For once in my life, I'm going to be brave.

Jax

~~~~~~~~~~

From the moment I lay eyes on her, that girl sticks out like a sore thumb. While everyone else in The Corner is dressed in dark workout clothes, she's draped in what looks like five or six layers of pink, blue and purple fabric. Her hoodie is candy-colored, dangling halfway down her thighs, and her leggings are white with blue polka dots. Even her icy blonde hair is tinted lilac.

Jesus. Just looking at her gives me a toothache. So fucking sweet.

Smack.

A fist collides with my jaw, snapping my head back, and I shake it off with a grunt. I deserve that. How often have I yelled at my students not to get distracted during a fight? How often have I lectured about the importance of focus?

Too many times to count—and usually, the second I step into the ring, the rest of the world melts away. Fires could rage and lightning could strike an inch from the ropes, and I wouldn't even notice it. Usually.

"Come on, Terminator." Dawson grins, his teeth bloody, and I know that glint in his eye. This joker's one of my oldest friends, and he's *thrilled* to see me off my game. His tattooed chest is all puffed up, and he's choking back laughter. "Get your head in the fight. Or has retirement turned you soft?"

Soft, huh? Alright.

My kick lands square in his gut. Dawson staggers backward, curling over, and his wheezing is louder than the music. My pulse thrums beneath my jaw, and I finish him with two more blows, eyes drifting to the candy-colored girl one more time.

Jesus. I'm staring at her again? I don't deserve this win—but Dawson's even more distracted than I am tonight, so fair's fair. And if I'm grinning as I smack his shoulder once we're done, if there's an extra swagger in my step as I leave the ring—sue me.

Soft. Cheeky prick.

He's lucky I'm fond of that face.

My towel dangles over the top rope, and I swipe it as I duck through. My whole body's slick with sweat, my chest heaving with exertion—and sure enough, the girl is still there, lingering by the ring with a few other watchers. The others drift away, laughing and shoving at each other, heading back to their own mats, but she waits. Watches me with something like hope.

She swallows hard as I approach, her lips pressing together in a nervous smile, and I force my constant scowl to smooth out. No need to glare at a newcomer.

Especially one as sweet as this girl. God damn, she's enough to give me diabetes.

"You lost?" I ask, scrubbing my face and throat with the towel, then flicking it over my shoulder.

She shakes her head, her wobbly smile stretching wider. "Nope. But, um—" She pulls her phone out of her pocket and shows me my own photo. "—You're found, Jax Sutherland."

…Ah.

Right.

She's one of *those*. The women who come here sometimes, looking for a tussle with a famous fighter. Wanting a taste of the Terminator. My gut sinks, the scowl settling back on my face, even as a treacherous part of me is tempted.

I've never laid with a fan before. Never been one for those kinds of perks. But *this* girl…

Well, she'd look like something special spread out on my desk, that's all. All that silky lilac-blonde hair draped over the scratched wood. Or maybe she'd let me press her up against the lockers, her little hands braced against the metal—

"You've got that wrong." My words are clipped, harsh with irritation. If she'd only taken the time to get to know me, to treat me like a human being and not a piece of meat, maybe all this electricity zapping between us wouldn't have gone to waste. As it is, I have my pride. "Whatever you're offering, I'm not interested. I don't screw fans. Now get gone, little girl."

Her eyes go wide. A pink flush crawls up her neck.

Could've licked that neck. Could've tasted her creamy skin, chasing that blush wherever it leads. Could've been a little nicer about telling her no, too, but what's done is done.

"I'm twenty one," she says. "A grown adult, thank you, and I'm not offering *anything* like that."

She's not? Her shy smile from before is long gone, and she looks… offended. A little hurt. Huh.

No, I don't like that. I don't like that at all.

Think I've put my foot in my mouth here.

"This is your boxing gym, right?" She sounds annoyed. That's fair. "Don't you teach people how to fight? I read that online—"

12

A laugh bursts out of me. It sounds strangled.

"I coach professionals," I tell her, but I barely hear myself. She really wasn't looking for a novelty lay? Is that why she's all closed off now, arms wrapped tight around her stomach? Like it's her instead of Dawson that I kicked in the gut?

Fuck, I hate that her pretty face has gone all pinched. First I let Dawson ring my bell, then I let my temper get the better of me, and apparently I'm *still* not done being an ass, because next I say: "I don't teach any random soul who wanders in off the street. You want to learn the basics, go down to your local community class."

She winces, arms squeezing tighter around herself.

The music changes, the tempo picking up, and all around us the sparring pairs go faster to keep up. They swing fists at each other; they lash out and kick. And with every smack of a landed blow, she flinches. So out of place.

Still, what is wrong with me? Why am I saying all the worst possible things? Why has she got me so on edge?

Because my being a prick is expected, sure. Everyone knows that fighters are brutes, and when we're not rude, some people even feel let down. Like they've been denied the proper experience. But I'm retired, damn it, and I don't want to live that way anymore, especially not when folks come looking for my help.

The least I can do is find her a good class. It won't make up for the way I've spoken to her, for the assumptions I've made, but it's better than nothing.

I clear my throat, scratching at my stubbled jaw as I say: "If you tell me your home area, I can recommend someone."

She puffs out a pained laugh, gaze dropping to the floor. And she's already turning on her heel as she says, "I'll do my own research. Thanks a lot, Mr Sutherland."

Ah, shit.

I grab her elbow before she's even made it two steps. *No.* She can't go. Not yet; not like this.

"Wait. Just—wait a second." Her arm is slender in my grip, and it hits me: she's so vulnerable. I could snap this girl with one hand. "Tell me something: why me?"

Because there are plenty of beginner classes in this city. Hell, there are plenty more advanced coaches too, and guaranteed, almost all of them have a nicer reputation than I do—with good reason, clearly.

So why did she come to *my* gym? Why force herself inside and across the room, when she's so obviously spooked by every single punch and kick? Why come to *me*?

My pretty interloper shrugs, her jaw set. And she can't be that scared of me, because the scowl she sends me is damning. "It doesn't matter now."

My chest aches. "Yes it does."

"Let go of my arm, please."

I drop my hold right away, but I stay close. Close enough to feel the body heat radiating off her; close enough to get a lungful of her blossom scent.

"Why come here?" My voice is low, urgent, because suddenly I need to know this answer. More than I need anything else in the world. I need this encounter to make sense. "Why ask *me* to teach you, huh? Everyone knows I'm a prick."

She shrugs again, but the fight's gone out of her. She stares across the room, her eyes unfocused, and says, "You didn't seem that way to me from the clips I watched." Didn't. Past tense. "And people do dumb things when they're desperate."

...Desperate?

14

My heartbeat slams in my ears.

She's desperate? As in… she's scared? Desperate to learn how to defend herself? Shit.

I grip her arm again, gentle as I can, and tug her to the nearest spare mat.

Forget everything I said before. Her first lesson starts now.

Casey

⸺ ❦ ⸺

I 'm getting whiplash from this man, and we haven't even squared off yet. First he stares at me from inside the ring, eyes hot and lingering; then he calls me 'little girl' and tells me to get gone. Now he's towing me to the nearest mat like that whole car crash of a conversation never happened.

Whatever you're offering, I'm not interested. I don't screw fans.

Ugh. Whatever, dude.

Like I'd ever give my v-card to a giant meanie like Jax Sutherland. Okay, maybe for a second back there, before he opened his grumpy mouth, I let myself wonder. I'm only human. When I saw the way he fought in the ring, so strong and sensual, muscles flexing and sweat sliding down his bare chest...

Yeah, I wanted to lick those beads of sweat right off him. Or follow them down his body. For a frozen moment, I turned into a complete horndog—and I guess he saw it in my eyes.

Doesn't matter. He was a jerk, and I would never have offered my body as some skeezy trade. So there.

16

"Take off your hoodie," the fighter says as we reach the mat, our sneakers sinking an inch into the suddenly softer ground. "You're too easy to grab hold of in that."

His thick eyebrows raise when I shake my head. This is not a man who's used to being told no.

But I have my reasons. "I wear this hoodie everywhere," I point out. "If someone *did* grab hold of me, I'd probably be wearing this."

And these lessons aren't just theory. Not to me. I need to know how to look after myself in real life—like when I'm walking home alone at night after a shift at the club, and it's so late my brain is fuzzy. When I'm bundled up in this hoodie against the chill and the streets are half empty, moonlight glinting off the damp sidewalk, and a shiver down my spine warns me that I'm being followed.

Well, Jax Sutherland doesn't like that. He looks like he's sucking on a lemon wedge. His bottom lip is cut through by an old scar. "You can't wear something else?"

I roll my eyes. "These are my clothes."

Because what am I supposed to do? Wear nothing but skintight jumpsuits for the rest of my life, and bonus points for slippery satin? I guess I'd be like a wet bar of soap if anyone tried to grab on, but I'd die of cold by November.

Jax Sutherland mutters something under his breath, but he takes me by the shoulders and moves us so we're standing square.

"Do you know the person you're scared of?" he asks bluntly. "Can you give me any pointers of what we're up against? Body type? Size? Speed?"

We. What *we're* up against. It's a turn of phrase, but it softens the hard knot of unhappiness in my belly—the one that's been lodged in there since he told me to get gone. I've carried all this fear alone for so long, for weeks now, and someone's finally on my team.

Thank god.

And maybe Jax was a jerk before, but he's trying now. He's giving me his undivided time and attention, and he made it pretty damn clear that he doesn't usually teach normies like me. When he heard I was scared, it's like a switch flipped in his brain.

Protective mode: activated. Hey, if I could pick anyone to have my back, anyone at all, I'd pick this surly fighter every time. Jax would grind whoever's stalking me into mincemeat, I know it.

"Sorry." I shake my head, and I really do wish I could be more helpful. The tension between us is slowly bleeding away, and I wish I could hurry it along. "I'm not sure what he looks like. But it's definitely a man."

Jax scowls even deeper. He's still holding my shoulders, his palms warm through all my layers of clothing. "And how do you know that?"

My hand drifts to my hoodie pocket. Am I seriously going to show him? Heat fills my cheeks, but yep, I raise a fistful of paper scraps between us. "From these."

Jax opens a palm beneath my hand, and I let a few scraps flutter down. They crinkle as he holds them up, squinting at the spiky handwriting. They're hard to read, some of them—and my stalker has a very loose grip on grammar—but a lot of them are… anatomical. It's a man, for sure.

As Jax reads, every ounce of warmth drains from his face. I hadn't even noticed him getting friendlier with me, but watching that deadly expression settle in… I shiver.

18

I'm glad we've settled into this truce.

Because he's super intimidating when he's angry. His shoulders swell. His chest puffs up bigger, too, still shiny with sweat, and his tattoos are so vivid against his tanned skin.

And for one crazy moment, I can't help thinking of the pigeons that live on the fire escape outside my studio apartment—the way they fluff up their feathers when they get mad.

I choke back a snort. Jax glares at me. "This is not fucking funny..."

"Casey," I supply. My shoulders slump, and I sober up. Forget the pigeons. No, it's not funny. It's scary and gross as hell. "It started at work, first. I sing in that lounge club by the river, the Blue Flamingo? Well, I found the first few notes in my locker there. Then a few got pushed under my apartment door, and left with my bag at the gym, and balanced on my grocery store basket when I turned away at the check out..."

I trail off. He gets the picture.

"He's following you." Jax looks ready to rip the punching bags from the walls and fling them out onto the street. He's breathing hard, eyes bright, and his pulse taps extra fast beneath his shadowed jaw.

I swallow hard. "Um. Yep."

"This prick," Jax says, holding up a fist as he squeezes the notes to a crinkled pulp, "is following you around the city. He knows where you work. Where you shop and where you live. And he wrote that fucking filth—"

"Okay, okay." I flap a hand, and my stomach churns so hard I feel queasy. "No need to spell it out. I know how much trouble I'm in; that's why I'm here."

"Have you been to the cops?"

Duh. "They were no help at all. I guess they're not interested

19

until *after* I've been attacked." My words are light, but I'm so scared that my bones ache.

Jax inhales sharply. "Not going to happen."

I huff. "Well, it might. That's why I need to learn this stuff from you—"

"And I'll teach you," the fighter says, and I don't think he even realizes he's kneading my shoulder gently. Squeezing me like I'm his personal stress ball. Damn, he seems even more worked up about this than me—and I've barely slept in weeks. "But it's not going to happen. Nothing bad will happen to you, Casey. Okay? I won't let it. You have my word. This asshole won't ever lay a finger on you."

Whew.

You know, he's not how I imagined my fairy godmother would be. Jax Sutherland is mean-looking and muscly, with close-cropped dark hair and a nose that's crooked from being broken so many times. His thighs press against his sweatpants, and his abs ripple with each deep breath he sucks in. A happy trail leads all the way from his chest down to his waistband.

But there's something soulful about those hazel eyes. And the hand on my shoulder is so gentle as it rubs and squeezes me through my hoodie, kneading my tension and fears away.

Okay. Jax wants to protect me? I'm not some prideful idiot, and I know when the universe is offering me a gift. I'm in. I'm so in.

"I'll hold you to that promise," I joke weakly, tapping his arm with my knuckles. It's that or fall to my knees, sobbing and clutching his leg with relief.

Jax's expression flattens. "You call that a punch? Jesus Christ, Casey. We've got a lot of work to do."

Jax

I haven't been in this part of town in years. It's too luxe, too fancy. The pale stone buildings all have fussy carved window sills and columns, and wrought iron railings on their balconies. Ivy climbs the walls.

In my faded jeans and black t-shirt, I'm out of place as I stride down the sidewalk. No empty bottles or gum on the street here—guess it's too crass to chew. Wine bars and boutique cafes line both sides of the road, and little tables have been set out in the fragrant evening air. Some have red checked tablecloths and jugs with flowers.

Hell, it even smells different here. Like the river is fresher, somehow, on this side of its banks. Every time I breathe in, I get a big whiff of spring blossom. Makes me think of candy-colored clothes and pale lilac hair.

People skirt around me as I walk, eyes widening with alarm when they see my battered face. I feel like a gargoyle that jumped off one of these fancy buildings and walked away, they're gawping so badly. No wonder I don't come to this area usually.

It's not like I can't afford the prices. The Corner does just fine, and I've got all those winnings from my days in the ring—I just don't like being ogled like some zoo animal.

Though… Casey didn't look at me like that yesterday. Like I'm an ugly motherfucker. She stared a little, sure, while I was circling Dawson, but with something like heat in her gaze. Heat and hope.

Until I told her to run along because I don't screw fans. God damn it. I've been cringing non stop since she blinked at me after that, all offended and surprised. Why did I jump to conclusions like that? Why be such a dick?

The real kicker is: after spending the whole evening with her yesterday, teaching her how to punch and kick and break a hold, I'd tear off my left arm if it meant getting a taste of that girl.

Doesn't matter. We smoothed all that over, and if I missed my shot with her… so be it. I'm still gonna take care of her.

After all, nothing else could tempt me into this part of the city. I'm more at home with the rough and ready atmosphere downtown: the smoke of barbecue joints and the roar of muscle cars. But Casey told me she works at the Blue Flamingo, and that she walks home alone at night, vulnerable and unprotected, so here I am.

Because: bullshit. That ends now.

I'll protect that girl until she sends me away.

Just ahead, four businessmen sit at the tables on the sidewalk, their ties loosened and their sleeves rolled. Suit jackets that probably cost more than my first motorbike are draped over the backs of their chairs, overpriced sleeves dangling toward the gutter, and they're sipping glass tumblers of scotch. Their voices are loud, drifting into the evening air as they bray about stock portfolios or summers at the cape or some other shit.

They clock me right away; stiffen in their chairs, but keep bragging to the street. One sneers as I pass, watching me over the rim of his glass, and I slow, raising an eyebrow. He chokes as he swallows, thumping on his reedy chest, and I roll my eyes before I walk on.

Not worth my time. And god, I hate people like that—people born with a silver spoon in their mouths, who think they're superior to the rest of the world when their palms are softer than a baby's behind. Never done an honest day's work in their lives, and yet because they can afford the prices on this block, they get to listen to a sweet thing like Casey sing.

Sure enough, the Blue Flamingo's only a few doors along. Two velvet ropes make a mini walkway to the entrance, and a bouncer in a suit and tie stands beside the door, arms folded over his burly chest. The soft sound of lounge music floats into the street.

I brace myself for trouble as I turn off the sidewalk, but he doesn't stop me or call me out for my faded clothes. The bouncer nods once, eyes skating over me then away, and goes back to frowning at the street.

Alright then. I duck inside, get ten steps down a plush corridor and past a coat room, before wheeling back around.

The bouncer glances at me again when I step outside, but he says nothing. This guy's made of granite—ex-military, maybe, with short, graying hair and a square jaw. He's here to do a job, cash a check, and go home.

I can respect that. And I'm not looking to waste time either, so I skip right to the point. "You know Casey, the girl who sings here?"

The bouncer nods, eyes flicking past me to watch a pair of suits walking past. "Yeah, I know Casey," he says, his voice like gravel. A smoker, I'd guess. Does he ever sneak one when he's out here all alone, the street empty? "She's a sweet girl. Dyes her hair."

I grunt, ignoring the territorial spike of annoyance at hearing another man call her sweet. It's not like she's mine, is it? I don't have any claim on her, and the bouncer didn't say anything out of line.

"Do you ever get guys come in here, asking about her? Any repeat customers sniffing around?"

The bouncer levels me a look. "Other than you, you mean?"

That's fair. He doesn't know me from Adam, and it's not like I arrived here with Casey. Hell, as far as he knows, *I'm* the asshole leaving her those notes—except I've never stepped foot in the Blue Flamingo before, and I'd stick out like a snowman in hell if I did.

"Think you'd remember me," I point out, gesturing at... well, all of me.

And the bouncer looks over me again, then nods. Hard to deny. So this time, when he speaks, he leans an inch closer, eyes still scanning the street behind me.

"Casey's got a few fans. It's expected, a pretty girl like that, and with that voice. She always gets a crowd. But I'd lay money that the person who watches her set most often is the boss, Mr Acheson. Always comes out of his office to see her sing, or so I'm told. More than twice her age, but since when has that stopped anyone?"

Speech over, the bouncer settles back on his heels, and from the clench of his jaw, the message is clear. He's done talking. That's all I'm getting from this brick wall.

"Thanks, man."

A tiny nod.

Sucking in a deep breath, I head back inside.

* * *

Casey's sitting at a table near the stage, a glass of water with ice and lime set on top of a single blue napkin. There's only one chair at her table—to stop randoms from trying to sit with her I guess—and she fiddles with the corner of the napkin as she watches the musicians play.

A big, bearded fella's giving a saxophone solo, shirt and waistcoat tight over the strain of his belly. The lights give his brown skin a purple sheen. He's good, I'll give him that—and Casey smiles softly as he trills through the notes, spinning her glass on the table.

No, I'm pretty sure *he's* not the stalker—but I'm still jealous as hell over that smile she's giving him. What is wrong with me?

I only met this girl yesterday, and already I'm like a territorial bulldog, inwardly snarling for others to keep away. So out of line.

The club is three-quarters full, with drinkers lounging and chatting, sipping at cocktails. The music is there for them to listen to when they feel like it, or they can let it fade into the background. Almost everyone's wearing a suit or a cocktail dress.

Something about them all chatting makes my teeth grind, too. When my girl sings, I want people to shut up and *listen*. But that's lounge music, I guess, and the performers here must be used to it.

And someone out there *is* paying attention to Casey, right? Too much attention.

I shake off my mood and weave past the tables and booths.

The air's hot in this room, hot and humid, and I burn up even warmer under my clothes when Casey spots me. She brightens, sitting up straighter in her chair, her palms pressed flat against the table like if she doesn't brace herself, she might run to me. Her lips form my name.

Fuck. Just yesterday, my hands were on her body. I held her trapped close to my chest, simulating a grab from behind; I wrestled with her on the mat. She was so soft and small and wriggly and goddamn, I need to plunge my whole head into one of these fancy ice buckets. Never mind if I get a champagne bottle in the eye.

"You came," she breathes when I grab a nearby chair and throw myself down at her table. Casey's staring like I'm some kind of miracle, and not a battered old grouch. "I can't believe you're really here."

"I said I would be." And Jax Sutherland keeps his word. Always. We all need something to cling to in this world, right?

These fancy fuckers might have the clothes and the looks and the knowledge to read a goddamn wine menu, but I have my integrity. Tit versus tat.

"I spoke to the bouncer," I tell her, keeping my voice low. Casey leans closer to listen, her dress rustling against her thighs, and I realize what she's wearing for the first time. It's a beaded dress that falls inches above her knee, the material silver and shimmery. She looks like a flapper or something.

Beautiful. So perfect. But...

"I—wait. Are you wearing heels?" Can she run in those without breaking an ankle?

"Of course." Casey wrinkles her nose. "I'm on stage, and I need to look the part. What do you want me to wear with a dress like this, Jax? Flip flops?"

I scoff. "In a chase scenario, flip flops would be even worse. At least in those heels, you can puncture a testicle."

Casey snorts, giggling into her glass. And I feel my face shifting as I watch her drink, ice clinking against the side, one of my arms draped over the back of her chair.

I'm... smiling. Huh. Doesn't feel natural.

But I've felt antsy all day being apart from her, and now that she's in my sights... I can relax. She's safe.

"The bouncer says your boss watches every time you perform."

"Mick said that?" Casey lifts one shoulder in a shrug. "Well, yeah. Mr Acheson watches all the performers at least for a little while. He needs to make sure we're on our game."

"But you more than others?"

Casey looks uncomfortable. She shifts in her chair. "I—I don't know. I've never noticed. But listen, Jax, after this song I'm on stage for an hour at least, so—"

"I'll stick around." The tension melts from her shoulders, and Casey beams at me. It's like being hit with a blast of sunshine. "And maybe I'll check out this boss. Discreetly," I add, when she looks worried again. "Don't worry. I won't cause you any trouble."

The saxophone trails off on stage and there's a smattering of applause—way less than this guy's talent deserves. I clap obnoxiously loud to make up for these other idiots, my palms slamming together, and Casey snorts before leaning over to peck a kiss on my cheek.

"Thanks for coming tonight," she says, her breath warm

against my cheek. "I can't believe you're really here, Jax. You're my hero."

I sit there stunned as she slides off her chair.

Yeah, I'll investigate alright. In a few minutes once I can stand up straight again.

Casey

I always feel a little bit naked on stage. Exposed, you know? You're up there under the warm beams of light, and the room beyond the stage is too dark to really see, and you only know there are people watching by the clink of glasses and the hum of conversation.

Some of the other performers don't like that people chat while we do our thing. But I like it—I can kid myself more easily that no one's really paying any attention to me, so it's safe to sing my little heart out.

The band strikes up, the opening notes to my set drifting through the hazy club, and I wet my lips once before I begin.

This is another weirdness: hearing my own voice carried by the microphone. The only other time I really *hear* myself like this is when I belt out show tunes in the shower. I'm always kind of surprised by the voice that bounces off the wet tiles and comes back to me: turns out I'm husky. Soulful. When I sing, I sound sweet and sad.

I wonder if Jax likes my voice.

It shouldn't matter, but my tummy clenches just thinking about it.

I want him to approve of me. My voice, my dress, my fledgling self defense skills. I'm a grown adult, damn it, but I've never wanted a man's praise so badly in my whole life. When he told me I was good at wriggling out of holds yesterday, I nearly floated up to the gym ceiling.

What is he doing out there in the darkness offstage? Is he still sitting at our table, scowling at me from beneath those dark eyebrows? Leaning on his elbows, with those arm muscles bulging from his t-shirt sleeves?

Or is he snooping around the Blue Flamingo? Checking out Mr Acheson like he said?

My voice wobbles as I picture our kindly old boss looking at me in an unsavory way. Tugging at that bow tie he wears. My throat goes so dry, I need to turn my head and clear it between lines.

Focus, Casey. I can freak out when I'm done with my set.

Though even in the humid darkness, half-blinded by stage lights, so exposed and vulnerable—tonight, I'm not really scared. Not with Jax here. Not after he promised to keep me safe in that gruff way of his.

I shift my weight, clutching the microphone as I sing, and I swear my nipples harden behind my dress.

Jax.

Will he walk me home tonight? Will he come inside when I invite him? And, please lord, will he stay the night?

Whatever you're offering, I'm not interested. I don't screw fans.

I grip the microphone tighter, my palm clammy. God. I need to get those kinds of thoughts out of my head.

* * *

"Something's not right." Jax strolls beside me along the river bank after my shift, the moonlight glinting off the water. Street lamps cast golden pools of light, and although it's a cool night, the air smells like flower blossoms. "I smell a rat, Case."

Stifling a squeak, I glance around the path by our feet. Then, idiot that I am, I realize what he means. "Oh. In the club?"

"Yeah." Jax's hands are shoved in his jean pockets, tattoos wrapping around his bare arms. He's not shivering, but goosebumps pucker his skin.

Too manly to need a jacket, huh? I bite my lip to keep from teasing him. I don't know him *that* well, even though sometimes he feels like my kindred soul.

"I checked your locker, but there were no notes. And I slipped into your boss's office while he was chatting to someone at the bar, but his handwriting doesn't match the ones you showed me."

Thank god. I suppose Mr Acheson could fake that spidery handwriting from the notes if he really wanted, but I prefer not to think about that. He's too grandfatherly, you know? And he gave me a box of toffee apples for Christmas. I scarfed them down in my PJs while watching game shows.

Nope, I don't even want to go there.

"Something feels off," Jax says again, and he sounds so frustrated that I nudge him with my elbow. I changed clothes after my set, and I'm bundled up in my candy pink hoodie, sky blue yoga pants and sneakers. Jax hid a smile when he saw me come out of the staff dressing room, all wrapped up in my bright colors.

The mean fighter's a secret softie.

"It's gonna be okay. You're here now, and for all we know, my stalker's already lost interest anyway. I haven't received a note in five days."

Jax grunts. Yeah, he's not convinced. "*I* wouldn't stop following you," he says. "You know. If I were a psycho."

Why am I flattered by that? I need my head checked. But I shrug and link our arms, so maybe he can steal some of the warmth that he's pretending not to need.

Trees line the river path on this side of its banks. My walk home from the Blue Flamingo takes thirty minutes along this scenic route—which I always take, since it's better lit. And as we make progress away from the fancy part of town, the path gets grubbier, the grass beside it more overgrown. Even the trees start to look shabby.

I don't mind, though. It's more real down this end of the path, somehow. Less polished and fake. And when these trees burst into bloom mid-spring—well, they can rival even the uptown city parks.

It's late. Long gone midnight. Does Jax mind being across town so late?

"Let's practice." I slip my arm free and dance away, walking backwards along the path. Raising both fists, I grin at Jax's wry expression. "What's the matter? You scared of me, tough guy?"

"More than you know," Jax says, so dry, and I don't have time to parse that because he's lunging forward, swiping for me. He's so strong and swift as he moves, almost like he's dancing rather than fighting.

I skitter out of reach, grinning wide, and shriek when my heel knocks an empty beer can. It scrapes over the path, and Jax laughs as he lunges for me again.

"You spook easy, Case."

"It was a scary can."

I'm already out of breath, even though we're not moving any faster than before. My heart's racing in my chest.

Jax lunges for me again, but he's not really trying. It's like a grown panther batting at a kitten. Toying with me.

"Come on," I goad him, darting forward to flick his shoulder. The muscle's so hard, it's like flicking a stone wall. "Don't go easy on me. I want to practice what I learned yesterday."

Jax's eyes gleam. "And what was that?"

"How to punch," I say, my feet slowing as I count on my fingers. "How to kick. How to go for the eyes—hey!"

Strong arms wrap around me, taking advantage of my distraction. I'm crushed against a hard, warm chest, my hands squished between our bodies, and this is where I'm supposed to fight my way free—but god damn me, I'm pressing closer, sealing our bodies together at every point I can reach.

"This is different," Jax pants. "Dawson never uses this technique."

He doesn't sound mad, though. His voice is rough in my ear, and I can feel his heart thumping beneath my palms.

He squeezes me closer. Tighter. I'm breathing hot against his neck, and our legs brush together as he keeps walking us down the river path. We must look crazy to any onlookers; like two drunks staggering home, clinging to each other for support.

"It's a new move. I call it the nipple cripple." My fingers snake between our crushed bodies, and I pinch Jax's nipple hard through his t-shirt. He makes a choking sound, then shifts our hips apart.

"Play fair," he grinds out.

"That's not what you taught me yesterday," I say, and it takes every ounce of my self control not to nip at the strong column of his throat. It keeps shifting as he swallows, and lord, I'd love to feel his stubble rasp beneath my teeth. It feels so good to sprawl against him like this. To be held. "You said to use every advantage I have—that nothing is off limits if it means keeping me safe."

"That's true. I did say that." The fighter sounds strained. Like he's mentally time traveling to The Corner yesterday and kicking his own ass.

We stagger a few more steps, and we're closer than ever. I can feel every fold of fabric between us; every thump of our heartbeats, rattling out of sync. Bet Jax isn't cold anymore, because I'm burning up like a struck match.

"So what's your next move, smartypants?"

Smartypants. I hide a grin against Jax's collarbone. He acts like he's so grumpy and tough, and then he goes and calls me something like that.

But: my next move. My next move.

Hmm.

…Okay, I didn't think this through. Because my arms are well and truly trapped now, and I can't lean back enough to headbutt him, and though Jax says anything goes, I'm not actually gonna bite the man who's helping me.

Sucking in a deep breath, I throw my whole body weight to the side.

I barely move an inch, trapped in the cage of Jax's arms.

"Nope," he says. "Try again."

We're marching backward all the while, inching our way toward home. Kinda wish we weren't, though. I never want this walk to end.

And maybe it's the thought of him leaving that addles my

brain. The thought of being lonely and scared and vulnerable again, lying awake until dawn, fretting over those horrible notes. Whatever it is, I'm in full, desperate dumbass mode.

"How about this?" I say, then rock up onto my toes. My front scrapes up Jax's body, over his sculpted muscles and hard edges, then I'm sealing my mouth to his. I kiss him hard and vicious, like it's all part of the fight, like I'm proving a point and not melting inside.

Jax grunts. His head bowed back with my kiss at first, like he was expecting some kind of trick—but after a brief moment, he kisses me back. Hard.

...*Yes.*

Thank god.

We stop walking. Stop grappling. Stop doing anything except cling to each other, mouths working together, both breathing hard in the moonlight.

Something splashes gently down by the river. A fish, maybe. Jax's stubble rasps against my cheeks, his tongue chasing mine, and I don't care. I don't care.

A whole ass alligator could haul out a few feet from us, and I wouldn't care until it started gnawing on my leg. Jax squeezes me tighter again, and I let out a blissed out sigh.

Somewhere along the line, my hands have grabbed two fistfuls of his t-shirt. This move was supposed to distract him long enough to make my escape, but now I'm here, I never want to step away.

So warm. So tingly.

I'm slick as hell in my panties right now.

Jax exhales against my mouth, his breathing shaky. He nips my bottom lip, sharp enough to sting—and reality crashes into my brain.

What the hell am I doing? What's he going to think of me after this? He already thought I was trying to screw him once, and this is how I thank him for helping me? By kissing him like I'm so desperate, I'd drop to my knees for him right here in the street?

It's probably true, but that only makes this worse. I should be ashamed of myself. Hell, I *am* ashamed.

"S-sorry!" I blurt out, staggering backward. Unlike earlier, it's easy to break Jax's hold. He doesn't fight to keep me close at all, and as he shoves his hands in his pockets, he looks resigned. "Got caught up in my move," I say, and it's such a weak excuse for my behavior, but at least it's true. "Worked though, didn't it?"

Jax says nothing for a long moment, turning to stare out at the river. He looks years older when he scrubs a palm over his face.

Then: "Yeah, it worked. But don't kiss your stalker, Casey. That's not a good plan."

No kidding. And I open my mouth to tell him that even *I* wouldn't be that dumb, but Jax is already striding off. I jog to keep up, and he doesn't slow down. At this rate, we'll be home in ten minutes.

"You gonna teach my killer move at The Corner?" I say, trying desperately to get us back to the light atmosphere from earlier. The camaraderie we had before I ruined it. My sneakers scrape against the path, and Jax finally slows when I nearly trip.

"No," he says shortly, and that's that.

We finish the rest of the walk in silence.

36

Jax

C asey lives in a fourteen floor walk-up, right up where the attic used to be. We climb the stairs steadily, and here's hoping her stalker isn't too fit, because it's probably harder to snatch a girl when you're all out of puff.

"You're not even breathing hard," Casey mutters behind me. She's bent low, red cheeked and irritated, and her sneakers smack against the steps as we climb. "The least you could do is wheeze a little, Jax. To protect my dignity."

I shrug, her bag strap gripped in my hand. I'm carrying her crap for her, aren't I?

Besides. Dignity is a lost cause tonight.

Can't believe I let her kiss me like that. Or no—can't believe I *fell* for it, kissing her back like she was everything I wanted in the whole world, like she fucking completed me, like all my dumbass dreams had come true. And all the while it was a trick.

Haven't been humbled like that for a long time.

I stomp up the stairs, my expression sour.

And I'm not mad at *her*, even though her little prank made a fool of me—but it's best if I get some distance from this girl, just as soon as she's safe from her stalker.

The floors in this building are scratched wood, the walls whitewashed. Someone's put a vase of dried flowers on one of the stairwell window sills, but somehow it makes the place look even more bare.

It's quiet, though, and back down in the lobby, the mail was organized into neat piles. So I see why Casey likes it here—I'd have killed to live somewhere this nice in my younger days.

When we reach the top floor, I hold out her bag while Casey rummages for her keys. She glances down at her door mat before letting us in, and there's new tension in her shoulders.

Scared that she might find another note. Scared to enter her own home. Christ.

Whoever's doing this to her… I'll pound them into a red stain on the sidewalk.

"Wait a second," I tell her, catching her by the arm before she goes inside. "Let me go first. Stay close, okay?"

She lets out a shaky sigh. "Okay. Thanks, Jax."

God. She doesn't need to thank me. I'm just glad I'm here, pushing her creaky door open and glaring into the shadows. Stepping forward, my whole body tensed.

Something crinkles underfoot. I freeze, heart pounding, and dread and rage churn in my stomach.

"Is it another note?" Casey whispers.

She's close, I remind myself over the deafening thud of my pulse. *She's safe.*

"Maybe." I glance around before squatting quickly, snatching up the curl of paper. I stand and hold it up, trying to read it in the light from the stairwell.

Spidery handwriting. Foul words about my girl. Check and double check.

"Oh," Casey says.

I crush the note so hard my knuckles ache.

"Forget it," I order, like it's as easy as that, jamming the stupid thing in my back pocket. "I'm here and this asshole will never get anywhere near you. I promise, Casey."

She's breathing fast and shallow. Her whole body is rigid with fear.

"He came to the apartment again—"

"But he didn't get inside," I say, reaching out to smack on a light. Sure enough, her studio is small and jumbled, but empty. "Close the door behind you. Lock it, okay? And stay right there while I check the closet and bathroom."

"That's a cleaning cupboard," Casey says dimly as she shuts the front door. The lock clunks shut. "You think I have a walk-in closet in this tiny apartment? That makes no sense."

Her voice trails off, and she slumps against the door. Too dazed with horror to keep talking.

I check the cupboard—nothing but cleaning supplies. A mop, a broom, a bucket.

The bathroom: a sink, toilet and mirror, and a tiny shower cubicle. Empty.

"We're good," I tell Casey, striding back across her studio to check the fire escape. "Anywhere else you think I should look?"

She shrugs, her cheeks pale. My chest hurts.

"Okay." I clear my throat, and I've never felt so useless in my whole life. "Hang tight. I'm gonna check the kitchen cupboards and look under the bed."

And even though I'm doing this to make her feel better, even though there's no way on earth a grown man could fold himself

39

into those cupboards, I run out of things to check way too fast. This studio's small, you know?

Nowhere to hide.

Finally, there's nothing to do but stand in the middle of the rug like an idiot and spread out both arms. But Casey lets out a relieved whimper, stumbling forward and crashing against my chest.

We sway together, and I've got her even tighter than earlier. Her heart's racing faster than a rabbit's.

"You must think I'm such a baby," Casey says against my t-shirt, her breath seeping warm through the fabric.

"No." I rub my chin against her hair. "Never, Case. Never. You're dealing with something you shouldn't have to deal with, that's all. And you're handling it like a champ. You told the cops, even though they did sweet F.A., and you went and fetched me, didn't you? You took a self defense class."

She exhales and nods, clinging tighter.

Thank god I didn't just send her away. Thank god.

"You got me wrapped around your finger in ten seconds flat," I tell her, because it's true and I'd rather make her laugh than protect my ego. "And now you have your own personal attack dog. A mean, ugly fighter who'll protect you every day of your life if you want. Not bad, right?"

Casey makes a tiny noise. Rubs her face against my throat. "You're not ugly," she whispers. "Or mean."

I *am*, but Jesus Christ, I want her so badly. I need this girl.

Not for sex—or at least, not only for that. No, I need her close, safe, *mine*. I need her happy and singing and dressed in bright colors, and sipping her morning coffee while she sits on my knee.

"It's late, Case. You think you could get some sleep if I stay?"

She blinks up at me, surprised, and I finally let go of her to raise both palms. I step back, chest drumming, and say, "On the sofa, obviously. You don't need to worry about that."

Her shoulders slump. Am I crazy, or does she seem... disappointed?

But: "Okay," Casey says. "Yes. Please stay."

* * *

It's a long night. The sofa's small and lumpy and I get a crick in my neck, and I can't sleep anyway. Too many thoughts racing; too much kicking myself to do.

Don't care, though. There's no place in the world I'd rather be, especially once Casey drifts off to sleep, her breaths turning soft and heavy.

The bed's pushed into the corner of the room, and she's under a pile of pink and purple blankets. Her lilac-blonde hair splays across the pillows, so glossy in the moonlight spilling through the open curtains.

The whole room smells like her. Floral and fresh.

And there's something I'm missing. Something that doesn't fit. Every time I shift against the sofa, that goddamn note crinkles in my back pocket, reminding me what's at stake.

Think, asshole.

I don't have bricks for brains, but I've always been more comfortable in my body than in my mind. If only I could punch my way to an answer—then Casey would be safe and happy by morning.

I shift against the sofa cushions, grimacing up at the shadowed ceiling.

She's close, at least. Calm and sleeping. Offering me so much trust, though I'm not entirely sure I deserve it. Oh, I'll never push her boundaries, will never step over a line, but I'm sure as hell lying here *thinking* about it.

Going over there and drawing those blankets off her. Stroking her hair off her cheek. Pushing her legs apart and settling my weight on top of her.

In my mind's eye, Casey wakes up and winds her arms around my neck; she makes that soft, scratchy sound and kisses me like she did before.

I rub my jaw, my whole body wired tight.

It's just a thought. It'll never happen.

And so that I don't make her uncomfortable—Casey will never know.

Casey

Saturday nights in the Blue Flamingo are always a little wild. It's the weekend, and all the men in expensive suits and well-heeled ladies are blowing off steam. The air's different too, hot and muggy from all the extra bodies in the room, shimmering with tension.

These people want to drink, fight and screw. In that order.

Even the snobby folks turn to animals on the weekend, designer wristwatches be damned.

The boss gives us livelier music on Saturdays—songs with a heavy beat and a faster tempo. I dance a little as I sing, shimmying my shoulders, the beads on my flapper dress sparkling in the lights.

Someone wolf whistles. The conversation is loud, punctuated by bursts of laughter.

I gulp down half a glass of water between songs, blinking in the blinding lights.

This time last week, I shook like a leaf in a gale all through my Saturday set, but tonight, I'm calm. Jax is out there. I'm fine.

He's been glued to my side for the last five days, only leaving to grab a few changes of clothes and to check in on The Corner. He's got some guy called Dawson running the place while he's gone, and though I said he didn't need to put his whole life on hold for me, Jax just gave me this *look*.

"You're more important, Casey," he grumbled, scowling like he was mad about it. Or maybe just mad that I didn't get it yet. "I'm not going anywhere until you're safe."

So. Yeah. I've got my own knight in faded jeans. He's wearing a black Henley tonight, tattoos wrapping around his corded forearms, and though I'm so grateful for Jax's protection... I'm dying here.

Every time he so much as glances in my direction, my belly twists and heat pools between my legs. Whenever his deep voice rumbles an instruction, my nipples bead and my cheeks flush. And that *kiss*.

I can't stop thinking about it.

Lord, I'm such a weenie. Whenever we're home alone at my place, bedding down for the night, all I want to do is crawl on top of the mattress and beg him to mount me like a wild animal. Instead, I've been stress baking cupcakes with pink and blue frosting, and spending way too long out on the fire escape, cooling my face in the breeze.

"Casey, ladies and gentlemen!" one of the musicians calls into his mic, and I wave before scurrying off the stage at the end of my set. The sound of the next act being introduced follows me all the way into the backstage area of the club, where the lights are dim and the sounds of the crowd are muffled.

I can hear my own breathing again. My heels click against the floor.

The ladies' dressing room is empty. Jackets hang on pegs around the walls, and pairs of sneakers have been shoved beneath the benches.

Jax is here, I remind myself as shivers race across my skin. *He won't let anything bad happen to me.*

He's probably hunkered on a stool by the bar, nursing a bubbly water and glaring at the nearest suit with pure disdain. My fighter has zero chill when it comes to blending in with the Blue Flamingo patrons.

Okay, let's move this along. Don't like being away from Jax for too long. I cross the room to the bank of lockers, yanking mine open and holding my breath as I scan my belongings. Tote bag, pink hoodie, blue checkered scarf. All present. No note.

The air leaves me in a gust. Good. Jax swept this whole room when we first arrived, knocking on the door with a pained expression to check there were no girls changing, and there was nothing funky going on then, either.

How much could really change in a few hours? I grab my white t-shirt and purple leggings from the tangle and toss them on the nearest wooden bench. I'm so paranoid these days. So silly.

I shimmy my dress over my head and hang it on a coat hook.

I'm hopping on one leg, one foot stuffed into the leggings, when the door creaks open behind me. Yeah, Jax always gets impatient after my shift and comes out to meet me here by the time I've changed. He doesn't like letting me out of his sight.

"Just a second," I say, trying not to think about how stupid I must look, hopping around on one leg in my underwear. *So* not the sexy, sophisticated vibe I'd prefer.

No answer.

I shove my foot all the way through—then pause, a cold sweat beading on my lip.

Jax always knocks first before coming in here. Always.

Fear closes my throat, and I spin around so fast I stumble. The graying bouncer, Mick—the man who always nods to me when I arrive for work—stands just inside the door. Watching me. Staring.

He's dressed in a black suit and white shirt, the buttons straining as his chest heaves. His eyes are narrowed, and he looks mad.

Mad enough to write those notes? Oh, you bet.

Fingers numb, I let the rest of the leggings drop onto the tiles. My arms twitch to cover myself, to fold over my chest, but I force myself to stand open and ready. I rock onto the balls of my feet, poised to move.

Well, at least you're not wearing that hoodie, a voice whispers in my head. *Jax will be pleased.* Near hysterical with fear, I choke back a laugh.

Because of course Jax won't be pleased. Jax will lose his freaking mind.

If he gets here in time, anyway.

Woof. Okay. My fighter has drilled these scenarios into me, over and over—but it's so different when it's real. When I'm facing down my stalker; a man who wishes me harm. No matter how much we grappled, I never felt scared with Jax.

My heart slams against my ribs. Shit, what if I pass out before this creep even tries anything? Like a bunny rabbit freezing in truck headlights?

I clear my throat, but when I speak, my voice is all crackly. "I'm not alone. There's someone here looking out for me."

Mick sniffs once, and he rolls his neck. Like I've pissed him off even worse. "I know."

He moves faster than a cobra, lunging forward, and I'm too slow, too weak, too scared. Panic fills my brain, my thoughts turning to white static, and then I'm crushed against another chest.

But this is nothing like the way Jax held me. Even when he banded his arms around me tight, not even allowing an inch of movement, he was careful. He never hurt me.

This asshole is crushing my ribs, squeezing all the air from my lungs, and already my eyes burn with tears.

"Shouldn't have found yourself a man," Mick growls, his hot breath misting against my hair. "I liked you better when you were sweet, Casey. Sweet and innocent."

Um, as if I give a flying rat's ass what this creep thinks of me. And that spike of anger cutting through my panic—it helps me reset. Helps me think straight.

What are my options here? One arm is truly trapped, but I could work the other free. There's no room to punch properly; no good angle to break this guy's nose. And he's so much bigger than me, strong and muscled and merciless. If there's one thing I've learned, it's to fight on my own terms. Lean into my skill set.

And I'm a wriggly mofo, and I have zero qualms about fighting dirty.

Well. Jax likes to remind me, over and over: when in doubt, go for the eyes.

"Settle down," Mick grunts, like he's not trying to squish me to a pulp. "If you keep quiet—"

He cuts off as I yank one arm free, then drive my thumb as hard as I can into the corner of his eye. It's wet and squishy and so gross I want to puke, but screw it: he's made my life a living hell. I hope his eyeball pops out and pings off the locker bank.

"Bitch!" my stalker roars, but the door slams open behind us, bouncing off the walls, and he's wrenched away before I can go for the other one. I stumble back in a daze, breathing hard as Jax punches the bouncer so hard he drops to the ground.

I swear, as his knees hit the tiles, the whole building shakes. But Jax doesn't stop, punching him again until he's on his back, and my fighter still doesn't let up. Not after ten hits, not after twenty. Not when the bouncer lies groaning and bloodied on the tiles, and not even when he lies still, barely breathing.

After a while, I tip toe forward, tugging on Jax's t-shirt. He's kneeling over the other man's chest, working him into a pulp, the tiles flecked with blood, sweat and spit. He jolts under my touch, but he stills, his back heaving.

"You should probably stop," I mumble through numb lips. "Don't want you going to prison for murder. Who'll check my kitchen cupboards for intruders then?"

Jax rocks back onto his heels, swiping an arm over his forehead. "Fuck," he mutters. "Fuck."

Tugging on his t-shirt a second time, I tell him: "Jax. Please, can we leave?"

Because I can't be in this room for a second longer. Can't look at the man on the tiles. I need a hot shower and a giant tub of ice cream and to sob into Jax Sutherland's chest on my sofa, stat.

His knees crack audibly as he pushes to his feet, and the fighter is stiff as he steps away from my unconscious stalker.

"This was his first and only warning," Jax announces to the room, even though Mick is long past hearing him. "We'll get the cops to come and scrape him up. He attacked you, so even they have to throw him behind bars now, right? And if they don't…" Jax's voice lowers. "He'll wind up at the bottom of the river. I swear that to you, Case. We know his identity now, and the cops might not believe in preventative action, but I sure as fuck do."

"Okay, Rambo." My joke is weak as hell, but it bursts the tension in the room, and Jax shoots me a soft look. His mouth quirks. Then he snatches up my clothes and leads me to the door with his arm around my shoulders, and I sag against him, so relieved.

Don't care if I'm half naked. Don't care that Jax is flecked with blood or that he's casually threatening murder.

I'm just glad the danger is gone.

Jax

I get her dressed and home, and she clings to my hand the whole way. Practically have to peel her off once we're in her apartment, nudging her toward the shower.

Sure, I'd give my left nut to join her in there usually, but tonight is not the night. Casey needs care. Love. Attention.

And I may be a battered old fighter, but I can give her all those things in spades.

I rinse my face and arms in the kitchen sink, then pace back and forth over her rug while I'm waiting, listening to the soft sound of drumming water through the bathroom door. Though small, her apartment is an explosion of blues and pinks and purples, a cluttered tangle of keepsakes and belongings, and being in such a *Casey* environment soothes the ache in my stomach.

She's safe. Unhurt. Whole.

Even though I let that asshole get so close. I promised he'd never lay a finger on her, and then *that* happened—

The shower stops in the bathroom. Soft bumps and rustling

noises mark Casey getting dried and dressed.

She should hate me. I swore to protect her, then slipped up in the worst way. Doesn't matter that I got there in time; there never should've been a clock ticking down at all. Fuck, *I* hate me. Once that creep Mick is dealt with, what excuse do I have for sticking around?

There was that kiss—but it didn't mean anything to her.

Could it mean something to her?

Pacing laps on Casey's rug, hands balled into fists, I can *feel* the bad mood crackling off me like static electricity. And I've faced guys bigger and meaner and stronger than me in the ring, guys who'd cheerfully hit me so hard that my brain dribbled out my ears, but I've never felt as vulnerable as tonight.

"Get your shit together," I tell myself under my breath. Marching back and forth, back and forth. "She's had a horrible night. She doesn't need to see this."

"See what?"

Casey stands in the bathroom doorway, toweling her lilac-blonde hair. She's bundled up in a pair of hot pink sweatpants and a tight white t-shirt, her small curves pressing against the thin fabric.

Are those—is she not wearing a bra?

Jesus. What the hell is wrong with me? Wheeling around, I direct my words at the dark window. "Nothing, Case. Just having a meltdown over here."

She hums, and it sounds like she's trying not to laugh. The towel rustles. "Me too. What's yours about?"

"Same thing, probably."

"That guy grabbing me?"

"Yeah."

"Uh-huh."

51

It doesn't mean anything that she's not wearing a bra. This is her home; she's getting comfortable. Not everything she does is some kind of coded message for me, and Christ, I think I'm going insane.

Haven't slept much lately. Haven't been able to workout like usual either, and those antsy feelings are piling up, putting my teeth on edge.

"Anything good out there?"

Casey's voice at my shoulder makes me jolt. God, this woman moves like a cat, but I keep staring out of the window. The street is dark out there, lit only by streetlamps and the occasional swoop of headlights. The neighboring buildings block the moon.

"Uh—no. Nothing going on."

She hums again, soft and husky. "There's nothing else for it, then. You're gonna have to look at me, Jax."

Ha. Shit. I turn around slowly, like a man facing his doom. And I am in a way—because here's this sugar-sweet girl who I've been craving for days, and she's about to run out of reasons to need me.

Casey's hair is damp and rumpled, and she's slung the towel around her neck. Her skin is pink and scrubbed raw, but her eyes are bright, crinkling as she smiles.

She pokes my chest. "You saved me back there."

I scoff, heart thundering. "Hardly. You had him on the ropes. And besides: it's my fault you were alone with him at all."

Just like that, Casey's face pinches into a scowl. She's fierce when she's mad. Like a little honey badger.

"Don't say that, Jax. You *did* save me, and you've been protecting me for days. You put your whole life on hold to do it. And if you never gave me those lessons—"

"Which I nearly didn't," I point out, but Casey goes on, ignoring me.

"—I wouldn't have known to jab him in the eyes. What were you supposed to do, huh? Superglue yourself to my side? I was alone for maybe five minutes, tops."

Hey, if superglue is an option...

"At least you didn't kiss him," I say, aiming for a joke and missing badly.

Casey's mouth twists. "Ew. No, I save that move for special occasions."

"Oh yeah? Like when?"

We're moving closer together. Has she noticed that? The way our bodies are drawn together, closing the gap between us without being told? It's like gravity, or something. Like slow-motion falling.

"Like when I have a big crush on a guy and I don't know how else to show it."

It takes a second for her words to sink in, and the whole time Casey stares up at me, chewing on her lip with nerves.

...Did she really just say that? That she *wanted* to kiss me? That it meant something?

Yes, she did, and now she's as taut as a rubber band, practically vibrating with tension as she waits for me to respond. And god, after this and everything that happened earlier...

Forget all those fighters who train at my gym. Casey is the bravest person I know, hands down.

And she squeaks when I lunge forward, lifting her against my chest. Her legs wrap around my waist and her fingers dig into my shoulders, clinging on for balance. The towel thumps to the floor beside us.

"A crush, huh?" Christ, why do I sound mad about it? The

words punch out of me, rough and low, and I'm scowling, our faces only a few inches apart. "I thought that kiss was just a sneaky move."

Casey laughs, breathless. "And *I* thought you weren't interested in whatever I was offering."

Touché.

We need to stop dancing around this right now. No more veiled confessions; no more halfway measures. All this uncertainty is gonna give me an ulcer.

"I want you," I tell her, squeezing her ass in both hands, and damn it, that's not the emphasis I want to give this moment. It's just where my hands have landed.

Whatever. I can be clearer.

"I want *this*," I squeeze her again, "but more than that, I want your heart. Your soul. Your first thoughts when you wake up in the morning, and your candy colored clothes draped all over my furniture. I want my ring on your finger and to hear you sing in the shower, and most of all, I don't want to leave here once Mick has gone."

Casey sucks in a wobbly breath, and I weigh my words.

Full honesty. Right.

"Actually, I wouldn't mind leaving this apartment sometimes. It's cute and all, Case, but mine has a bathtub and a king-size bed, so—"

She grips the sides of my face and kisses me like her life depends on it.

My heart lifts. My pulse races. In the back of my brain, there's a whole chorus of angels playing trumpets. Because Casey's *kissing* me, and it's not a move this time or something we can take back, and when her tongue nudges against mine, I forget how to breathe. The room spins, and I stagger to the sofa and sit us down.

"Case," I say between kisses, her little hands yanking at my shirt. "Wait. Are you sure you want to do stuff tonight? After what happened earlier?"

She answers by tugging my head back by the hair—and searing kisses along my jaw.

Jesus, I'm harder than rock right now. I could do a zero-handed press up.

"I mean it," I tell the ceiling, grinding my teeth as she squirms in my lap. "If you're traumatized or whatever—"

Casey snorts. "'Or whatever.'"

"Casey."

She huffs and pulls back to glare at me. My hands are on her waist, thumbs rubbing at her stomach, and when did they get there?

She's rumpled. Exasperated. Her damp hair has left see-through patches on her white t-shirt.

No bra, my caveman brain chants. *No bra. No bra. No bra.*

"I am fine, Jax Sutherland." Casey tilts her head. "Would *you* like to stop?"

I would literally rather die, and I tell her so.

"Then would you stop being a weenie about this and join in? I'm doing all the work here—"

"Right." I yank her t-shirt up over her head, freeing those perfect tits, and Casey laughs loud and bright as I fling it at the wall.

I cup her. Squeeze her. Pinch her rosy nipples. Suck on the left one—then the right so it doesn't feel left out. And all the while Casey's panting and squirming, tugging on my hair and hissing at me to keep going.

Perfect.

She's so goddamn perfect. My brave girl.

And I'm going to make her mine. Going to take her apart, piece by piece, until she's sobbing with pleasure in my arms. Going to get her addicted to me, the way I'm already hooked on her.

I kiss every inch of her that I can reach: her mouth, her neck, her shoulders. Her collarbone and her chest. And then I urge her to stand above me, feet sinking into the sofa cushions on either side of my hips, so I can kiss another part of her.

"Been wanting to do this since the first minute I saw you." My teeth scrape against her hip as I drag those sweatpants down. No underwear. A sigh gusts out of me, and I rub my stubbled jaw against her thigh. "I bet you're sweet as honey down here, too."

"Um." Casey grips my shoulders for balance as she kicks the sweatpants off her ankles. "Let's talk about unrealistic expectations."

"You talk. My mouth's busy."

"But Jax—"

I lick a stripe up her inner thigh, and Casey chokes off, trembling. "Yeah? You want this?" I growl, steadying her by the back of her thighs. Casey whispers something, and it sounds like *screw it*.

"Yeah." She sways forward an inch, bringing her body closer. "I definitely want this. Keep going."

Casey

❧

Okay, I have no clue what I'm doing really, but I jabbed a man in the eyeball today. I can do anything. And as soon as Jax's hot mouth nudges between my legs, his tongue swiping along my seam, all the worries bouncing around my brain go quiet.

Alright. Not *all* of them. But what are the chances I actually taste sweet down there? I just showered, sure, but I'm a human woman, not a candy factory.

He doesn't seem to care, though. The fighter groans, ragged and deep, and his eyelids get heavy as he licks me again. Gripping both hips, he shifts me even closer and tilts his head, his tongue probing deeper.

God.

So hot. So wet and tickly. So freaking *good.*

This was worth the wait. And I can't believe Jax said all those things, can't believe he wants this as much as I do—but you'd better believe I'm jumping all in.

He did save me, no matter what he thinks. But more than

that, he's made me feel brave and strong and capable for the first time in maybe my whole life. Jax Sutherland believes in me, and he's such a force of nature that I can't help agreeing with him. Believing in me too.

My legs wobble, and I let slip a moan as he sucks on my clit. He grunts in approval, and he's acting like such a caveman. I love it.

Love *him*. Love this. Love the rasp of his stubble against my inner thighs and his hot breath between my legs and the pleased, low sounds he keeps making. Love his scarred, swollen knuckles and his firm grip on my hips.

His chest rumbles beneath me, and this feels so good, I'm lightheaded.

"Jax," I hiss, hips bucking as his tongue dips inside me. Nobody's *ever* been in there.

The fighter growls, rough and low, and jerks me closer. Licks me deeper. My legs are quaking so badly now that he's holding me up, supporting my weight like I'm no more than a feather.

Oooh god. I can't... this is... I'm gonna...

"Jax," I squeak, then my teeth clamp shut. I go rigid, twitching and pulsing beneath the steady strokes of his tongue. My whole body's burning up. I'm on fire.

Then my knees buckle and I'm gathered against his chest, lowered onto his lap, hushed and kissed and soothed by a man with three breaks in his nose. He strokes my hair off my face like I'm so freaking precious, and I can't bear it.

Fumbling for his jeans button, I curse my stupid fingers. Why won't they work properly? Why is my body working against me *now*, when if I don't feel this man inside me soon I might die?

"Easy," Jax says, batting my hand away, and his mouth is

curved up in amusement. He flicks the button open easily, tugs his zipper down—then pauses.

"Oh my god," I say, writhing in his lap with impatience. "Get it out. *Please*, Jax. I need to feel you. Need to screw you." Need to stop babbling like a lunatic, but the fighter grins and takes out his cock.

He leans back against the sofa, one hand around his cock, one arm spread along the sofa back. So arrogant. So confident. So filled with male satisfaction that yes, his shaft is big and thick and it makes my mouth water.

Ugh. I love it.

"You're unbearable," I tell him, shifting forward on wobbly knees. "Look how smug you are right now." Stealing a swift kiss, I notch him at my entrance.

"Who wouldn't be smug?" Jax says, his hips twitching up the tiniest amount. Clearly fighting the urge to pound up into me. "I've got the most beautiful girl in the world in my lap, and she's staring at my cock like it's the best gift she's ever received."

It is. Along with the rest of him.

"Should've put a bow on it," I say, sucking in a sharp breath as I sink down the first inch. And god, I can *feel* Jax's laughter. It vibrates right through me, tingling where our bodies join, and as I take him deeper, the sensations only get more intense.

I can feel his heartbeat, throbbing in his shaft. Can feel every breath lifting his chest, my palms braced against his body, and can feel his warmth seeping into my front.

We're so connected.

My throat tightens, and I swallow hard.

I will *not* be the virgin who cries on her first time. I will not get overwhelmed by love and hormones and all these freaking sensations, and god, the *stretch* of him. Gah.

"That's it, Case. Sit down on it. Yeah, good girl."

Heat floods my cheeks, and my belly twists. And Jax raises an eyebrow, watching me closely, his palms smoothing up and down my sides.

"You like that, huh? You like hearing you're a good girl?"

Yes. Holy crap. Why do I like that so much?

I've never especially cared what other people thought of me before this man. Never wondered if someone liked my clothes or my hair or my voice. But then I met Jax, and lord, I want to be *his* good girl. No one else's.

"You're so tight and slick, baby. Gripping me like a vise. Christ, this is the best thing I've ever felt, you know that?" Hands stroke up and down my flushed back. "I'd die for this, Case. I'd kill for it."

I'm whimpering now, working myself down his length, and my skin is damp with sweat. My nerve endings are tingling, and when Jax brushes one nipple with his thumb, I almost lose it.

"Oh, god." My forehead drops onto his shoulder. My ass meets his lap. He strokes a big, scarred hand up and down my spine, hushing and soothing.

"That's it. We're there, Case. We're there. You're doing so well."

Not well enough. I want *both* of us to lose the ability of speech.

When I rock my hips forward, he chokes out a groan.

And yeah, this is what I want. Jax's muttered curses and those big hands, roaming over me like he owns me; the creak of the sofa as our bodies rock together. My neighbors can probably hear this, but I don't care.

I'm having an awakening here.

And when Jax thrusts up into me, bouncing me on his thighs, I grin, exhilarated. Every time his shaft pushes into me, it lights up all my nerve endings, one-two-three.

"Holy shit," I breathe, thighs burning as I work myself over him, clumsy but so into it.

"Yeah," Jax mutters, then he leans forward and licks my throat. He sucks a kiss there, too, and speaks into my skin. "Holy shit."

The air around us gets muggy from our panting. We're both hot and sweaty, grinding out bodies together.

Jax leans back briefly to let me tug his shirt off, flinging it into a pile with mine, and when we come back together, we're skin-to-skin, baby. My eyes roll back, it feels so good.

His chest is so strong and muscly. The dark hairs of his happy trail tickle my front, all the way down my belly, and his stomach's clenching with each breath, his abs shiny with sweat.

I want to lick him all over. Want to rub this man all over my bare body until I smell like him forever, scent-marked like in all those bonkers werewolf romances I read when I can't sleep. Want everyone to know that he's *mine*, and I'm his.

I'm so his.

"I love you," I grit out, remembering way too late that I didn't respond to his declarations earlier. Guess I thought it was obvious, but that's no good. Some things need to be said out loud—maybe even yelled over the city rooftops. And I spoke quietly, but I *know* Jax heard me because he curses, fingers digging into my side, then he's pounding up into me like a desperate man.

"Case. Fuck."

He's a man of few words, but I do love him. And I wouldn't change a thing. Not his surly manner, nor his constant scowl, and especially not the secret, gentle way he is with me.

When he's not trying to pound my brains out, anyway.

We don't last all that long. It's been a hell of a day, okay? And we're both working out a week's worth of pent up emotions, all the bottled longing, and hey. It's my first time. Maybe after a few tries, I'll get better at drawing it out, but for now the tension's twisting tighter and tighter in my belly, and I'm getting lightheaded, and my breaths are coming shallower, and I—

I bury my face in Jax's throat, groaning like crazy as I come. Should I be embarrassed about that? Probably. I don't care, though.

Because Jax curses one last time, his filthy declarations bouncing off my studio walls—then he drives himself home and swells inside me. Fills me with hot, endless spurts.

It's so animal. I feel like something off the Discovery channel, especially once we've both caught our breath, eyes hazy, and all I want to do is wriggle on his lap and spread his seed around inside me. Paint the walls.

Must be more tired than I thought. And now that the bubble of tension has finally burst, now that we're slumped in each other's arms, I can't stop giggling. I press my face against his shoulder, and yeah. I'm definitely lightheaded.

"You're nuts, Casey," Jax says fondly, stroking my back again.

"Yup." I nip his collarbone. "And I'm yours."

His relieved sigh is the best thing I've ever heard.

Jax

ten months later

The Corner is packed full of sparring pairs, lights shining down onto the action while traffic rumbles past in the street outside. Music throbs from the speakers on the wall, but the main sound is still the smack of knuckles meeting flesh. The grunt of a kick in the gut. The rhythmic pounding of punching bags, and the creak as they dance on their chains.

I fold my arms beside the boxing ring, stifling a smirk as Dawson circles the young woman in there with him. He's got his hands up, fists clenched, and he's ready on his toes—in a fighting stance, basically. But every time she dances close, swiping at him, he lurches backward like he might get an electric shock if they actually touch.

"Come on!" she yells, lunging for him again. Her dark braids are tied back in a bun, and her white t-shirt glows against her brown skin. "Dawson, what the hell! You promised you'd teach me this stuff."

He shakes his head mutely, still backing away, and shoots me a pleading look.

Nope. He got himself into this mess, and he can get himself out of it. Shouldn't have agreed to teach his pretty little neighbor, should he? Not if he's so scared to even lay a finger on her.

It's like he doesn't trust himself. Well, I remember that feeling. The first night I met Casey, it took all my earthly focus not to pin her to the mat and just *rut*. Wanting a woman that badly does a number on a man.

"Boo," Casey says behind me, poking me in the ribs. I turn, grinning, and sling an arm around my wife's shoulder, then nod at the pair circling each other in the ring.

"Look familiar?"

Casey squints at the non-fight… then snorts. She smooths a palm over her t-shirt clad stomach, her candy pink hoodie parted around her growing bump. "They'll figure it out."

"Let's hope so. How was your day off?"

"Good. How's the gym today?"

"Good."

We trade goofy smiles, because yeah. Everything's good. No trouble in sight. Casey's stalker is ancient history, and she's been headlining at the club, and her kindly old boss is eager to have her back just as soon as she's ready once the baby comes. The Corner's doing well too, for what it's worth.

Dawson makes a retching noise in the ring, but we both ignore him. Casey burrows into my side. "You want to go a few rounds?"

"And get my ass kicked by my pregnant wife?" I kiss her temple, my heart so full. "No, thanks. I have a reputation to uphold around here."

"As a jackass," Dawson puts in, then curses and stumbles back as his sparring partner lunges. She nearly gets him, her fingertips brushing across his chest, and an odd expression flits over Dawson's face before he dances back. A moment of longing.

Yeah. We turn away, and I steer Casey through the maze of mats toward my office. They'll figure it out. Because what's the alternative? Missing out on *this*?

My wife drags me into a searing kiss before my office door has even shut.

No way. It's a no-brainer.

These are the things worth fighting for.

unhook the headpiece.

Jack and Dan stumpis in their curses and stumbles back at his spin interpretation... When...he nearly gut him, no more

... Days on a lad, before in Donkeshaul. A moment of surprise.

Soon. Went... a sweat at his coat deep through the unzipped ... button down burly office ... Up ... I unge again. Became who's ... the afternoon? Mishap on, and ...

Why do you stop, the rip's warm? back from my office door
I've seen that.

No way. It's no-mans...

has seen that enough to pull fighting long.

II

Hard Knocks

Description

H e's gorgeous, muscled, and a giant pain in the ass.
But when I ask for help, he comes running.

I swore I'd keep my distance from my tease of a
neighbor. He's always pushing my buttons—always trying
to get a rise out of me.

But when a spate of break-ins makes me nervous, Dawson is
the one I go to for self defense lessons. Can't believe *he's* the
one I want at a time like this, but I can't help it. All my instincts
cry out for him.

So we spend time together. Alone, sweaty time. And the more
I'm around this man, the harder it is to push him away.

Are we doomed to bicker and fight forever? Or could we have
something different?

...Something great.

Lara

~❦~

Another break in. Only three buildings down this time, and they emptied that place out, leaving poor Mr Markopoulos with nothing but his battered old sofa and a layer of broken glass and debris on his apartment floor. Whoever did it even drank the poor guy's case of ouzo from when he visited family back in May, spilling a giant, sticky puddle on the floorboards.

Ugh. People are such animals.

And it's the fourth burglary on this block in two months. Must be a local crew, and I *hate* that thought.

It's making me suspicious, and now I second guess every person I walk past in the street. Like: *is it you? Or you? Or you?*

I don't want to be a paranoid jerk. Sure, this neighborhood is a bit rough around the edges, and when I moved here I declared it was just until I finish my grad program and get a pay rise. Figured I'd bounce right out of here as soon as I could swing a bigger rent, off to a part of the city with more trees and fewer graffiti tags scrawled on the walls.

But I like it here. The people are friendly and the food places are great. And it turns out I don't have to be on guard around here the same way I do at college—always on my best behavior, always saying the right thing. Never stepping a foot wrong or giving people reason to doubt my intellect.

This neighborhood is my home, the only place I truly relax, and there are only two flies in the metaphorical ointment.

Fly number one: the break ins.

Fly number two...

Well, I gust out a long breath before I knock on his door.

There are muffled sounds inside my neighbor's apartment. A creaking floorboard; the clatter of something tossed on a table. The low drone of a TV or radio. So I *know* he's home, but it's just like Dawson Reynolds to take forever to answer the door. He's been nothing but a giant pain in the ass since the day I moved in.

I still think about it sometimes. The shit-eating grin he gave me as he carried my heaviest boxes up the stairs, barely breaking a sweat; the way his muscles bulged and his eyes twinkled. At the time I was flustered, stammering my thanks, but then he called me that stupid nickname—

Dawson tugs his door open wide and smirks. "Princess."

My hands ball into fists. I blow out a slow breath and force my fingers to unclench, smoothing them down my pinafore dress.

"Hello. Um." You know, I *rock* my seminars at college. I'm always well-read and thoughtful; I make powerful arguments that impress the lecturers. Then I spend ten seconds around this man, and I can barely string a sentence together. God, I hate him. "Do you have a minute?"

Dawson's smirk stretches wider and he gives a mock bow,

his dark hair flopping over his forehead. It's shaved close at the sides, long on top—the same shade as his short beard. "Of course, Your Highness."

Breathe, Lara. In and out.

I will not let this man push my buttons. I am better than this.

But Dawson's got a dish towel flipped over one shoulder, like Mister Domestic. As though I interrupted him cooking up a gourmet storm. I bet he keeps it by the door to look busy when someone knocks; bet he never picked up a spatula in his whole damn life.

He probably lives off boxed mac and cheese and those instant ramen packets. He has that energy.

"You're thinking evil thoughts about me, princess," my neighbor drawls, leaning against his door frame and folding his arms. "I can always tell. You get this little scrunch in your nose."

I do *not*—

Dawson grins as my hand flies up, feeling along the bridge of my nose, and okay. This is why I've barely ever knocked on this man's door before.

I can count the times on one hand, actually. The first time, he'd accepted a delivery for me while I was out. The second time, I was getting everyone to sign a bon voyage card for Mrs Klimp. And the third...

No, I think that's it.

I try very hard to avoid Dawson Reynolds.

But desperate times lead to desperate measures. And four break-ins lead to the most humiliating request of my life.

"I need self defense lessons. From you."

Dawson blinks. For once, he's stunned to silence, and I should relish this moment, because it sure as hell won't come around again soon.

"I'll pay," I say quickly before his mouth starts working again. "And we can do it here, or in that gym you go to. The Center?"

"The Corner," Dawson murmurs. He's still staring at me, green eyes wide.

He hasn't said yes. Why hasn't he agreed? I *know* he takes on odd jobs between stunt work. He gets bored otherwise.

"Why?" Dawson says at last, and his voice sounds rougher than before. I clasp my hands, goosebumps prickling over my bare arms.

Figured that would be obvious. "There's been another break in—"

"No," my neighbor interrupts, and damn him, he's smirking again. Fully recovered from his shock. "I mean, why *me*? Lots of people could teach you self defense. Do you even realize what you're asking?"

Oh, please. It is hardly rocket science. "I need to learn to defend myself, Dawson, and you are very conveniently located—"

"You're asking me to spend time with you."

He is maddening. But Dawson leans forward, and I'm suddenly very aware that we're alone on this floor, our two doors the only sign of humanity. Obviously this building is full of people, but right now, we might as well be stranded on Mars together. Two souls alone in the universe, where anything could happen.

"Time alone," he murmurs. "Talking. Touching. Not killing each other."

I cough to clear my throat. It's tight suddenly, my heart fluttering in my chest. Must be indigestion.

And why is he making such a big deal about this? We can be

alone, no problem. We're alone right now, with zero casualties!

"It's purely professional," I say.

He grunts, like he disagrees.

"It *is*."

Dawson tilts his head. "Whatever you say, princess."

Gah! I throw up my hands, already turning on my heel, because this jerk is right. Plenty of people can teach me self defense.

I don't know why I wanted it to be him so badly. Sure, he's familiar, and he feels very safe and homey in an irritating sort of way—but those things aren't important. I need lessons, that's all. A simple business transaction.

Nothing about Dawson Reynolds is simple. This was a terrible idea.

"Wait," my neighbor says, snagging my elbow before I can stomp back to my own door. "I'll do it. No need to go all huffy."

"I am *not* huffy, and if I am it's only because—"

"We'll start at The Corner. Plenty of witnesses there." Dawson's thumb rubs against my elbow, and I try desperately to ignore that tingly sensation. "Tomorrow evening at seven. That sound good?"

I nod stiffly.

He lets go.

And I take a giant step away, tugging my clothes straight even though they're already pristine.

Dawson's expression flattens, and he rolls his eyes before stepping back inside his apartment. "You can use that revulsion tomorrow, princess. It'll help you fight harder."

I'm not repulsed. I'm just… I'm flustered, that's all. Whenever this man's eyes are on me, my whole body flushes warm, and I can still feel those tingles where he touched my arm.

So I open my mouth to thank him, to smooth this over, but Dawson's apartment door swings closed.

Thump. Right in my face.

Charming.

Dawson

I get to The Corner fifteen minutes early, agitation making me walk faster than usual. I stomped the whole way here, marching like I was setting off to war, and in a way, I am.

An hour or two with my prissy little neighbor. It's more time than we've ever spent together, and with good reason: the two of us were built to push each other's buttons. So usually, she can't wait to get far, far away from me—and I've worked hard to bury my disappointment over that.

It doesn't matter. It can't.

Me? I'd love to hang with Lara. She's prim, yeah, and kind of a know-it-all, but in the best way. Any idiot can see she's got a huge heart to match that beautiful brain.

But even though I liked her immediately when I met her, she did not return the favor. And life's too short, you know? No point in trying to coax people to like you. Either they're into you or they're not, and a man's gotta have some pride.

But I pluck at my black t-shirt, wrinkling my nose at the sweat beneath, and hope I don't stink by the time Lara gets here.

God. I've got no dignity when it comes to this girl. She raises her hoity-toity nose and asks me to jump, and all I can say is: "How high?"

So I'm pissed off by the time she arrives at The Corner, picking her way through the mats and looking so damn out of place. Even in workout gear, she's neat. Bet she ironed those blue leggings.

Her dark braids are tied in a big bun at the nape of her neck, and her white t-shirt glows against her brown skin. Even though she's covered up, those hourglass curves are on full display.

Fuck. The longing swells in my chest, same as it always does: a giant wave crashing through my insides, leaving splintered wreckage in its wake. She's so goddamn beautiful. But then Lara spots me, her whole body going tense, and I push all those feelings away.

She doesn't like me. She never has. So, as she said last night: this is a business transaction, nothing more.

I'd have taught her this stuff for free any time, even before the break-ins, never mind all the bad blood between us. But this is better. Keeps things clear.

"You're late," I say when she reaches me, nodding at the big clock on the wall. It's seventeen seconds past the hour, and I'm obviously teasing her, but Lara frowns like I've insulted her honor.

"I reached the entrance in plenty of time."

Ever the stickler. Will she ever let her guard down around me, even a tiny bit? I sigh, scratching my beard. Signs point to no.

The Corner's busy this evening, despite the sticky summer

heat. All the doors and windows have been thrown wide open to the sidewalk, and giant fans are dotted around the walls, wheezing hard as they work overtime. But it's still scorching hot in here, the air humid enough to chew on, and sweat pours down all the fighters' faces as they spar. Lara looks alarmed as she peers around.

"You don't have to worry," I hear myself say. "No one will bother us. Jax runs a tight ship."

Lara's plump mouth twists, but she says nothing.

Right. Fine. I jerk my head at the boxing ring in the center of the massive room and start leading the way.

"Wait, we can't go in there." My neighbor trips after me, hurrying to keep up. She darts around each mat and pair of sparring fighters, giving them double the space she really needs to. Her sneakers are dazzling yellow and white. "People will stare."

"No, they won't."

They've all got better things to do than looky-loo at a beginner lesson. This crowd is dead serious about their training, and sometimes they don't even stop to watch the big guns fight, like Jax and Sarge—and okay, me.

Baby's first punch? Hardly gonna draw an audience. But Lara's shoulders are rigid, her lips pressed in a line, and she glares daggers at me as I hold the ropes apart so she can duck through.

It's like she thinks I'm punishing her or something. Putting her on display. But people honestly aren't gonna give a shit what we're doing, and this way, I don't have to worry about my cute neighbor getting caught by a stray kick. The ropes will keep everyone at a good distance, and we'll have more privacy than if we grabbed a random mat.

Try telling that to Her Highness, though. She shakes her arms out in the center of the ring, stretching her neck left and right, and she's clearly picturing me in a crumpled mess on the ground.

"Easy, tiger." I stand in front of Lara and grip her gently by the shoulders. "You can wipe the floor with me in a second. Let's start with your stance."

* * *

Lara's a quick study. Figured she probably would be, what with that giant brain of hers, but head-smarts don't always translate to a body in control. It's depressing the number of clever folks we get in here who can barely throw a punch.

They never last long. Ego's a powerful thing.

But Lara watches each move I demonstrate, frowning with concentration, then mimics it almost perfectly each time.

"Drop your shoulders. Yeah. Watch where you're putting your feet."

She takes notes well, too. Corrects her form with zero complaint, glancing over at me with those big, brown eyes as though to ask: "Like this?"

Yeah. Like that.

I turn around and snatch up my water bottle, chugging down three mouthfuls. The heat and the walk here—and okay, Lara—are getting to me. My throat's dry as a bone.

But I promised my neighbor a lesson, so I get back in there and hold up a pad. "You're gonna punch this. Okay, princess? As hard as you can. Don't forget your form."

Is she picturing my face as she pummels the pad, smacking it with her boxing glove? She must hear the idle thought somehow, because Lara shoots me a mischievous smile between hits.

My heart lurches. I stagger back a step and she follows, still pounding the pad.

She's good at this. A natural. And that *smile*—

I can't think straight. That must be why I say it.

"Okay, now lose the gloves. We're gonna run some scenarios."

Bad idea, I think, as she unwinds the wrist strap and tosses one glove, then the other. Lara shakes out her fingers, blowing on the knuckles. They must be sore.

Bad idea. Bad idea.

Because I've got no business grabbing Lara, play-acting like some creep. Self control can only take me so far. If I lay hands on her... if she sees something in my expression, some treacherous flash of longing...

"Actually." She's squaring up to me, bouncing on her toes. Her chest jiggles under her t-shirt, and I hate that I notice it. Goddamn lizard brain. "Maybe not. Maybe we should run some kicking drills."

"Hang on. What are the chances I'm going to use some fancy kicks in real life?" Lara points out, super reasonably. They're slim as hell. "Let's do the scenarios."

But...

With a sinking feeling, I realize: I can't grab her. I can't.

Some part of me knows, deep down, that I'll cross a line if I do. The animal part of my brain will take over, and I'll hold her too tightly; I'll crush her curves against my chest. I'll let slip how badly I've wanted to touch her, because there will be no way to hide how my body responds.

Nope. No, thank you. I have exactly one shred of dignity left, and I'm gonna protect that little thing.

"Let's go." Lara lunges for me, swiping with a fist, and I dance back out of reach. Over at the side of the ring, Jax has wandered over to watch. I flip him off, my face hot.

Lara falters, glancing over too. "Who is that?"

"Jax Sutherland. He owns the gym. Don't worry, he's not watching you; he's trying to freak me out."

And it's working, asshole. Can Jax see all the messy, tangled feelings I've been dragging around for my neighbor? We've been buddies a long time, so… probably.

Ugh.

Goodbye, shred.

"Let's do those kicking drills."

"No, come on." Lara lunges for me again. I dance back. "You promised you'd teach me this stuff, Dawson!"

Yeah, I did—and I took her money, too. But fear has me by the throat right now, and I don't trust myself. Because what if I hurt her? I couldn't live with myself. Or what if she realizes how I feel about her, and then she's too horrified to live near me anymore?

"I paid you," Lara points out, fists still held up, and even though it's true, it tenses my neck. I glare at her, mouth sour, and spit out my next words.

"And I'll give it back. I'm not doing this."

The sounds of the gym are so loud: the throbbing music and pained grunts. The smack of fists meeting flesh, and the squeak of sneakers against the floor.

Lara's arms drop, and she stares at me, bewildered and hurt. The air's thick between us, the tension almost too much to bear.

"Do you hate me that much?" she demands. "So much you won't even touch me? After all this, you really won't teach me to defend myself?"

Do *I* hate *her*? No, she's got that all wrong. It's the other way around—it always has been. And I shake my aching head, opening my mouth to speak, but she's already squeezed out between the ropes, striding away across the gym floor.

Shit.

I rub the back of my rigid neck, watching her go. It's for the best. For the best.

Never should have started us down this road.

Lara

I have this routine when I'm upset, but it's gonna seem insane. Don't judge me too badly, okay? Because I'd been living in this building for six weeks before I learned through the laundry room grapevine that Dawson Reynolds is a big-time stuntman.

That's why he's so fit and agile. Why he fights so well. He's in tons of Hollywood blockbusters, filling in for the lead actors in their fights and car crashes and cliff dives. His muscles are famous.

I found Dawson's profile online. Lost my mind a tiny bit.

Then started this new habit: whenever I'm low, I pop a big bowl of buttery popcorn, crack a lemonade, and settle in to watch my neighbor on my TV screen. Sure, I'm mostly guessing when it's him in the frame and when it's the actor, but I like to think I can tell.

Dawson Reynolds has a very distinctive set of shoulders. And his butt? Extremely toned.

I squint at the lemonade label, a little shocked at my own

horn-doggery. Nope, this is definitely non-alcoholic.

The butt in question tumbles past on screen as Dawson flings himself off a motorbike. He tumbles over and over on a tarmac road, falling with style—but it's the famous actor who stands up and winces into the camera.

Does it bother Dawson that most people wouldn't even realize he's on screen? Flying under the radar like that, an uncelebrated talent?

I grunt and shove a handful of popcorn in my mouth. Who cares? My neighbor is a giant jerk, as he proved again today. Don't know why I'm even watching this. I need a new feel-better routine.

A knock on the door interrupts my zen. I pause the movie and heave off the sofa with a sigh, popcorn rustling as the bowl shifts. Can't a girl catch a break? All I want to do is drool over my jerky neighbor, take a hot shower, and slide into my freshly laundered sheets. Who needs me at 9pm?

Dawson glowers as I yank the door open, still dressed in the black shirt and gray sweatpants from the gym. He smells like fresh sweat, and is it weird that it smells kinda good to me? I inhale sharply, sucking up those pheromones without thinking.

We're standing close. Alone again. Dawson holds up a folded stack of worn bills—my payment for our disastrous session.

"Brought your money back."

I reach out, my mouth twisted. Why do I feel guilty about this? He's the one who refused to teach me the good stuff! But we did do an hour of drills before that.

"Keep it," I say, dropping my hand. "I'll just trash you in my online review."

Dawson's eyes crinkle, his expression warming. Is this it?

Are we joking together, finally? Bet if I glance back at my window, there are pigs flapping past outside.

"I don't hate you," my neighbor says quietly, though there's no one around to overhear us. "That's not what happened back there, princess."

Whatever. *Something* clearly went wrong, but I'm over it. I huffed out all my frustrations while power-walking home, and that soft look he just gave me has short-circuited my brain. There's no other excuse for the way I hold the door open wider, rocking back a half step.

"I'm watching one of your movies. Wanna join?"

Dawson blinks over my shoulder at the screen. His green eyes are startled. "One of mine? Like… on purpose?"

Ha. "I like to play Spot the Jerk."

Dawson snorts, and he follows me inside in a daze. He sets the folded bills on a side table near the door, like I wouldn't notice. My belly flips, and why does that make me so flustered? Maybe because I can kid myself that he's fussing over me.

"What markers do you look for?" he asks.

"Big attitude. Big head." Toned butt. "That scar on your left forearm."

We collapse together on the sofa, and this is so surreal. We should be sniping at each other, trading insults and glares, not passing snacks. Dawson accepts the popcorn bowl, digging out a big handful.

"Yeah, I broke that arm seven years ago. Stunt gone wrong. It happens. Needed two surgeries for that one, and I've got metal pins here," he tilts his elbow, "and here. At this point, I'm almost more metal than man. They hate me in airport security."

God. How many bones has he broken making these movies? Does he *like* pain? Holy hell.

"I could not do your job." The movie starts up again, but I dial down the volume. Some insane part of me wants to keep chatting. "I'm such a wimp about getting hurt."

"Good," Dawson says softly, and when I risk a glance, he's got that warm look in his eyes again. It's like a palm stroking over my bare skin. I shiver. "I'd hate if you got hurt like that, princess."

Princess. There it is again—but I don't mind the nickname so much this time. It sounds less mocking and more... fond. Maybe even reverent.

Have I been reading this man wrong all along? Months and months of strained interactions flicker through my brain, and I tense up while watching the mental slideshow. So many curt comments. So many rolled eyes.

So, no... no. Things have been bad between us, no doubt about it.

I watch as Dawson chews a mouthful of popcorn, his big body sprawled over my sofa like he owns it. He wriggles to get comfortable, letting out a pleased sigh, and I swear he's like a stray cat scoping out the new home he's about to invade.

And maybe things could be different from now. Maybe we could upgrade to frenemies.

"If you pee on my rug, I'll be so mad," I tell him.

Dawson jolts, staring like I'm insane. "What? Why would I—oh. Marking my territory, huh?"

I raise an eyebrow. And he melts back against the cushions, somehow even more smug than before. My chaotic neighbor *likes* the idea of staking a claim.

Well, it's a comfy sofa. Who can blame him?

"This is the best part," Dawson says, pointing at the screen. "It's one of those moves that *looks* really simple, and most movie watchers wouldn't really register it. But if I was in a bar full of stuntmen right now, they'd all buy me a drink."

I watch obediently, wincing as the body on screen plummets over the side of a building... only to catch himself by the fingertips on a window ledge.

"You know how hard that is?" Dawson crows, stealing a sip of my lemonade.

"Stop bragging! You are such a boaster." I sound mad but I'm grinning, and when Dawson jostles me in the ribs, my grin only gets wider.

"How else am I supposed to impress you, princess?"

Like this. Being sweet; being fun. Not mocking me for watching his movies like a creeper, but rolling with it instead. Who knew Dawson Reynolds could be so kind?

And *flirty.* If he slides any closer to me on the sofa, pressing our sides together, we're gonna blend into one super-organism.

I wouldn't hate it.

But he doesn't mean anything by it—I know that. Wild, funny stuntmen like Dawson Reynolds don't go for bookish prudes like me, and that's just a fact. I lived through high school, you know? I understand how this works.

But for a minute, as our bodies lean together, vibrating with laughter as we point at the screen...

I'll let myself pretend.

* * *

Here are the rules of the truce: Dawson and I smile at each other when we pass by the hall. We fetch each other's mail. We hold doors open when the other person's arms are full, and we chat idly about the weather. In short, we're good neighbors.

But we do not, I repeat, do *not* mention the failed self defense classes. I bury that hurt way deep down, stuffing it between my ribs, and only let myself wonder about what went wrong when I'm alone.

Hey. I'm not saying our system is perfect. Because even though that rule spares us an awkward conversation or two, the memory of him refusing to touch me kind of... festers. Every time we linger together in the lobby, exchanging polite words, the tension grows a little thicker.

Why wouldn't Dawson touch me? He sat next to me on the sofa without complaint. Hell, he smushed our sides together, normal social rules be damned. Like he couldn't get close enough, no matter how he tried.

So why call off our class? Did I do something wrong? Did I suck really badly and not realize it?

Why?

The unanswered questions follow me like wasps, buzzing and circling my head. They sting, too, whenever I let myself wonder for too long.

When there's a fifth break-in on our block, I think about asking Dawson for help—then dismiss the idea immediately.

Been there, done that.

Got the raggedy t-shirt.

Dawson

The Corner has been my happy place for years. We did it up with our bare hands, and that's a heady feeling. I knew Jax before he bought the building to start his own gym, and I was there from day one: painting walls, clearing out junk, laying the special heavy floors. Hanging rows of punching bags around the huge room.

I worked on this place day and night between movie shoots, swapping my usual exercise regimen for the hard graft of building something from scratch. There's no better feeling, I swear, and every time I come in here, I get a little hit of pride.

I even helped build the boxing ring in the center—Jax, Sarge and I tackled that project in a single weekend. Around midnight on the first night, we broke for beers and a noodle box delivery, then got stuck back in. Crashed in sleeping bags on the floor, then got back to work before breakfast.

Great days. I peer around The Corner, my vision hazy as I stare back through the years. They fly by so fast, I blink and miss 'em.

That was the weekend I met Sarge for the first time. Thought he was a mean-looking motherfucker, and I wasn't sure about him at all, but Jax pulled me aside and told me to give the other guy a chance. Said he had his demons, no doubt about it, but who doesn't? And beneath all those glares, he's got a rigid sense of honor.

It's true. And the three of us have been thick as thieves ever since, because when you get the same splinters as another man, you're bonded. Pure and simple.

I weave between mats and sparring pairs, searching for Sarge now. It's a Friday night, and the gym's only two-thirds full, because people have dates to go on. Beers to drink. Mistakes to make before they're back in work on Monday.

Night's falling outside, and the gym lights shine bright overhead. Music thumps from the speakers on the wall, and someone on this block must be cooking barbecue, because the scent drifting in from the street makes my mouth water.

Sarge is impossible to miss. The Scot stands head and shoulders above most other men here, and his shoulders are broad enough to catch on door frames. I asked him once exactly how tall he is, but he just rolled his eyes.

One of these days, I'll get a step ladder and a tape measure, and *then* we'll know.

"Hey, man." We catch hands; thump shoulders. Sarge doesn't crack a smile—but then again, he never does. Does he even know how? Does his face work that way? "Why are you lurking over here?"

He's dragged a mat away from the others, and now he's just standing here with his arms folded. This guy has that eternal patience that I sorely lack: it's like storms could rage and continents could drift, and Sarge would still be standing here, gazing across the room.

"Private lesson," he mutters, his deep voice gravelly with lack of use. Our man here is not a chatty Cathy.

"You?" I snort, and Sarge sucks his teeth, but he's amused too. You can tell by the infinitesimal crinkling of his eyes. "What did Jax promise in return? Another cook-out at his place?"

Sarge turns to me slowly. "He said you'd lose your shit and I could watch the show."

Huh? That makes no sense. Why would I care about Sarge's private lesson?

My gut realizes before my brain does, dropping to the floor.

"No." I wheel around, searching the crowd… and there she is. Lara. My beautiful neighbor strides across the gym, checking the time on her phone, dressed in black leggings and a green t-shirt. Her braids are tied in two low buns, and it's so fucking cute that I could howl.

She looks up, and her whole body tenses when she sees me. Her mouth turns down. The rest of the walk to us, she comes more slowly, visibly wary.

"Sarge?" she asks the other man when she reaches us. He grunts. She blows out a relieved breath and puts out her hand. "I'm Lara. We have a lesson tonight?"

"No," I say again. No one listens, and the sight of Sarge's huge, scarred hand wrapping around Lara's makes me want to tear the nearest punching bag off the wall and fling it into the abyss.

They shake hands. He asks what she wants to learn. She explains about the break-ins.

"No," I repeat louder, like a stuck record. "No, this can't happen."

By now, Lara's written me out of her personal universe. She

won't look at me, won't hear me. We're back to square one, and hell, I don't blame her. Why am I making such a big deal of this?

I *want* her to be able to defend herself. More than anything in the whole world, I want her safe.

But does it have to be Sarge teaching her? Big, brooding Sarge, with his growly Scottish voice that all the female fighters giggle about? Sarge with the thick auburn hair and square jaw that is always rough with stubble, no matter how often he shaves?

Sarge? Really? *Him*?

This has Jax fucking Sutherland written all over it. And his wife Casey. I bet all of them are in cahoots.

"We'll warm up with some drills," Sarge says, jerking his chin at a mound of boxing gloves and pads in the corner of the mat. The look Lara shoots me as she brushes past is pure acid.

"You don't need to watch," she hisses under her breath. "I don't need a babysitter, Dawson."

No, she doesn't. Neither does Sarge.

But I can't leave them alone together. I can't.

For the first twenty minutes of her lesson, I pace along the edge of the mat, bristling with agitation. I *know* I'm being the world's biggest prick, and that I have zero right to hover like this, but my caveman brain is riding me hard.

It's saying: *mine*. Lara is mine, and Sarge shouldn't lay a single finger on her. What if he hurts her by mistake? That big yeti body must be hard to control. Or what if they touch each other, and sparks fly, and they both decide they like it?

What if I'm about to watch my buddy and the girl of my dreams fall in love?

Jesus, this stomach ache. I prop my hands on my hips,

breathing through the discomfort as I pace.

I couldn't stay in this city if they got together. I'd have to leave the country—start a new life as a shepherd in Albania or some shit.

"You're handling this well," a voice says behind me.

Jax. This joker. I ignore him, pacing faster as over on the mat, Sarge demonstrates how to throw your body weight into a punch. Lara nods and watches him so seriously, giving one hundred percent of her focus.

So studious. So perfect. Fuck.

"I mean it," Jax says. "Very dignified."

Bullshit. I'm like my mom's house cat whenever another tom sprays too near the back garden. My fur's all spiky, and I'm practically hissing at everyone. So humiliating.

"If he hurts her..."

"He won't," Jax says, stepping neatly in front of my path when I turn back. "Stop pacing, man. You'll wear a groove in my floor."

"You did this," I mutter, but I stop at last and fold my arms. We both watch the lesson together, Jax with a sunny smile, me with a scowl. Is it just me, or do Sarge and Lara look good together? They're both flushed from the heat, lines of sweat trickling down their throats and disappearing beneath their clothes.

What I wouldn't give to lick that off her.

"Could've been you, Reynolds."

Coulda, woulda, shoulda. But I blew it, didn't I? Because I was scared Lara would notice my stupid crush; that she'd sense the constant craving I have for her. Figured the second we got too close, all my emotions would spill everywhere and stick to her like radioactive goop.

She deserves better and I knew it. But this is *not* what I had in mind.

"I taught Casey this stuff when we first met," Jax says idly, picking a fleck of dust off his black t-shirt. "It's a powerful experience to share with someone if you have that... connection. Very intimate, you know? Borderline erotic."

My throat is so tight.

"Don't you have female coaches?" I grind out. Sarge doesn't even teach normally, for God's sake. Says it's too much time spent with humanity. "Couldn't you have assigned her someone else?"

"Yup." Jax smirks, so damn pleased with himself.

My temples throb. I pinch the bridge of my nose, and as Lara tosses her gloves to the side, the two on the mat squaring up to grapple, I can't watch anymore. It's none of my business anyway.

"Well, this has been fun." No, it hasn't. This has been like scouring my insides with a wire sponge. "But it's Friday night, so..."

"Hot date, huh?" Jax yells behind my retreating back, and as I flip him off over my shoulder, I suck in a deep breath, count to five, and remind myself why I like these idiots.

Or I try, anyway, striding across the gym toward the street. Right this moment, it's hard to think of a reason.

Lara

I'm not surprised when Dawson comes out to meet me when I get home. These stairs creak like we're in an old wooden ship, not a city apartment building, and it's easy to hear everyone's comings and goings.

I've puffed my way up six flights of stairs, my muscles sore from my self defense lesson, when Dawson's apartment door jerks open.

He sticks his head out first. Damp, dark hair, slicked back from a shower, and the beard that despite myself, I still want to pet. Then the rest of his body follows. He's dressed in black sweatpants and a wine red t-shirt that clings to the muscled planes of his chest.

"Lara." Folding his tanned arms, my neighbor watches me approach. "How was your session with Sarge?"

"Good, no thanks to you. How was your hot date?" I fire back.

Ever since the gym owner yelled those words after Dawson as he left, I've had a sickly knot in my stomach. Did he really go on a date tonight? Must've gone badly, right, if he's home alone now?

Or, God, did it go *really* well, and that's why he showered? I swallow thickly, fumbling my water bottle open.

Dawson glowers at me as I swig a mouthful—and why the hell is he mad? I've done literally nothing wrong. He wouldn't teach me self defense, so I found someone that would. I won't apologize for that.

"You didn't need to go to Sarge. I'd have taught you that stuff."

Ha! I splutter mid-drink, thumping my chest as I cough. Dawson steps closer, one hand raised, like he's ready to give me the Heimlich maneuver or something.

No white knight needed, thank you. I wave him back, my eyes burning.

"We tried that, remember?" I rasp between coughs. "You didn't want to touch me."

"That's not what happened," Dawson grinds out, a muscle leaping in his jaw. He's so rarely angry that I never get to see him like this: vibrating with frustration. Normally, he's pure sunshine and charm, joking with the mail carrier and helping our neighbors move heavy furniture up the stairs. This is kinda fascinating.

Annoying, but fascinating.

"Did you know that a tendon stands out in your neck when you're mad?" I tap my throat. "Right here. If the little old ladies from the laundry room could see you now, you wouldn't be their favorite anymore."

Dawson rolls his eyes and yanks us back on track. "It's not that I didn't want to touch you, Lara. Believe me, that's not the problem."

97

Ugh. What does that even mean? Why can't he be clear for once? I'm so tired of second guessing; so tired of nursing hopes that will never take flight.

"Goodnight, Dawson."

Our corridor is quiet, my steps muffled by the dark carpet. My key scrapes loudly as I slide it into the lock.

"Wait," he says behind me. I turn the key and push the door open, but then his voice lowers. "Please, Lara."

I stand in the doorway, mouth twisted. Right there, my serene, tidy, *predictable* apartment awaits me.

No nasty surprises in there. No charming neighbors who blow hot and cold. Just a warm shower, my cozy PJs, a bowl of crisp green apples on the counter, and a sociology paper to write. Bliss.

"It's not that I didn't want to touch you," Dawson says, each word bitten out like it pains him. "It's the opposite problem. I wanted it too much. I thought that grabbing each other like that... being pressed together... I might lose my head."

Oh. Um.

Wow.

My heart's thumping so loud, they must hear it three floors above us. I need to turn around and *see* him, so I can picture this confession forever, but my legs won't work. My eyes are glazed, staring at my sofa as he goes on.

"I shouldn't have acted like that at The Corner." The floor creaks as Dawson steps closer, his heat washing over my back. "The first time *or* tonight. You have every right to be mad. And you don't have to do anything with this information, princess, but I can't stand the thought of you walking around, thinking I didn't want to touch you. Thinking that I hate you. It's... you couldn't be further from the truth."

Need more water. God, my throat's dry.

My hand shakes as I raise my bottle, and Dawson huffs a sad laugh, his breath stirring against my neck as I drink.

"You're really not going to talk to me, huh?"

Nope. The whole time we've known each other, talking has got us nowhere. I snap my water bottle closed and draw in a ragged breath.

"Stand right there," I tell him, turning slowly on the spot. Dawson gazes down at me, statue-still, eyes burning with emotion. "Just... shut up for a second. Let me try something."

"An experiment?" Dawson rasps as I brace my free hand on his chest. It's so strong and firm, his heart thumping beneath my palm. So alive.

I wet my lips. "Yeah. I'm testing a theory."

Because we've been circling each other for months, sniping and griping, but after that little speech, it's finally beginning to dawn on me... maybe this isn't hate we're feeling.

When we both get flushed and tense around each other, bodies humming with life... maybe it's something else. Something *good*. Something I've been longing for.

I rock up onto my toes, pressing against Dawson's chest for balance.

"Lara," he whispers, and he sounds so awestruck, I can't help but smile.

"Don't distract me. I'm a woman on a fact-finding mission."

He nods and braces both hands on my waist. "Yes, ma'am."

And I have to crane my neck to reach him, my thigh muscles throbbing, but when our lips brush together...

Okay, this is embarrassing. I swoon.

I sway forward against Dawson's chest, kissing him harder, gripping his t-shirt—and he groans with encouragement, gathering me close. With those big arms around me and his head tipped over mine, I've lost all structural integrity. I've turned to goo.

"Lara," Dawson says again, muttering my name between kisses like a prayer. "*Lara*. God. Finally."

He's fresh from a shower and I'm sweaty. The floorboards creak beneath us, announcing our every move to the whole building, and the light flickers on the wall, but for all that... it's perfect.

Better than I ever dreamed.

Every place this man touches me, my body sings to life. And every time he breathes my name, my heart thumps harder in my chest.

He wants me. I want him.

And we've been fighting this for so long.

Why? Why did we do that? When his beard brushes against my cheeks, it's the best thing I've ever felt. His spicy-clean scent makes my head swim.

But when Dawson turns us, backing me into the nearest wall, my heartbeat stutters. I falter, losing our rhythm and turning our perfect kiss clumsy.

Because he moves like a man with experience. A man who knows what he's doing—and who wants to do it with me. And I've never cared before about being a bookish prude, but now it's like I'm about to sit a test I forgot to study for.

Panic churns in my belly. My palms are damp.

"You okay?" Dawson murmurs, kissing gently down my neck. He's not pressed against me anymore, his body hungry and demanding. He felt me draw back and stepped away too, always the gentleman.

Gah. What if he doesn't want to teach me from scratch?

What if deflowering me would be a chore? What if I ruin this?

My cheeks burn hot from embarrassment, and nothing's even happened yet.

Come on, Lara. Don't be a coward.

At least tell him.

"Um," I say, and my neighbor leans back to watch me closely, hanging on my every word. I could tell him. I should tell him. But instead I say: "I'm hungry. And I need a shower."

Something flickers behind Dawson's eyes—disappointment, maybe. But he nods, and he steps all the way back, waving an arm at my open doorway.

"Okay. Goodnight, Lara."

"Goodnight."

I scuttle inside my apartment, slamming the door too hard. It's a long time before the floorboards creak outside.

Dawson

I spooked her, no doubt about it. My cute, shy, oh-so-serious neighbor finally kisses me, and what do I do? I flatten her against the nearest wall, rutting against her body like an animal. Don't even have a good excuse; my instincts took over. Lara deserves so much better.

Such a jackass. This is exactly what I was scared about with the self defense lessons: something about that girl makes me lose my damn mind. I go pure caveman.

If I'd kept my head, I'd *know* that Lara would want things to go slow. That she'd want dates and picnics and nights at the movies, slowly warming up to the idea that we don't have to fight all the time. We can choose a different path. Together.

Instead, I rushed things. I let slip how badly I want her, and she got spooked.

That's fair. *I'm* unnerved at the way she rules my body; the constant craving I feel for her. The sheer goddamn hunger. Who wants that?

* * *

Moonlight spills through my open drapes, casting a silvery glow over my apartment. It tints the black leather couch blue, and casts weird shadows from the trophy cabinet in the corner. The awards in there are for stuntman stuff mostly, and a few fights too, and usually they give me a little glow of pride, but tonight I feel hollow.

What's the point in a bunch of stupid awards if I can't impress the one person who matters most? What's the point in cleaning my apartment like a madman every few days just in case she comes over, when she's never once stepped inside?

Blargh. I'm no good late at night: I go all crabby and sour. My normal good mood bleeds away with the sunset.

"Lighten up, jackass," I mutter to myself, weaving between the sofa and the coffee table to stare out over the city lights. Could switch a lamp on, I suppose, but that wouldn't go with my tortured idiot vibe.

Tomorrow. I'll fix things tomorrow.

I'll take Lara the prettiest bunch of flowers I can find, and I'll explain to her that we can go as slow as she likes. That I'm grateful for every second I spend with her, no matter what we're doing. I will prove to my girl that I'm more than animal instincts, damn it.

And if I'm lucky—the luckiest guy on the planet—maybe she'll give me another chance.

There's a soft knock on the door.

I stand still for a long moment, back tense, breathing deep. Didn't even hear the floorboards creak out there. Did I imagine it?

Another knock, even quieter this time. I cross my apartment

in five strides and fling the door open.

"Oh!" Lara jerks back, staring up at me with those big brown eyes. The lights are off in the corridor too, and we're alone together in the gloom. "Jeez, do you have to answer the door like that? You scared the crap out of me."

I'm lightheaded with relief as I take her hand, pulling her gently inside my apartment. She's here. Thank god. "Shouldn't knock on a door if you don't want it opened."

"Is that from a fortune cookie?" Lara squints as I flick on a floor lamp, her braids tied in a high bun. Guess she couldn't sleep either, but god, those prissy little white pajamas, with the shirt collar and the tiny shorts and everything...

I'm in heaven.

"Probably." I nod at my kitchen doorway. "You want a drink? Think I've got peppermint tea somewhere, or whiskey, or there's coffee if you're feeling really buck wild."

She must be, right? Else why has she knocked on my door at 2am?

"Dawson, have you seen this?"

Lara holds up a glowing rectangle, and I frown into the glare of her phone. It takes me a second to process what I'm reading, then my eyebrows bounce up my forehead.

"Yeah, they caught them," Lara says, breathless with excitement. "Earlier tonight, like, six buildings down. I'm surprised we didn't hear any sirens. No more break-ins! For now, anyway."

"For now," I agree.

Huh. This is good news. Why am I not more pleased?

Maybe because for a moment there, I thought Lara rushed over here in the middle of the night to see me. Because she couldn't wait until morning. Because she feels the same desperate need to be near each other that I do.

I scrub the back of my neck. "Thanks for telling me, princess."

This is fine. At least she's happy to be alone with me, right? There's trust here. That means there's hope. And once I've brought her those flowers, once she sees how serious I am about her...

"That's not the only reason I came over," Lara says, tossing her phone across the room onto the sofa. It flies in a glowing arc then disappears between two cushions.

"Oh yeah?" I stare at the spot where her phone light snuffed out. "Then why—"

I'm cut off by a shoulder in the gut, Lara's small, soft body barreling into me. She locks both arms around my waist and charges me back toward the wall, and I'm too shocked to do anything but grunt, staggering backward.

"Lara!"

She hooks an ankle around my knee and buckles my leg. Shoves on my shoulders and tries to get me to kneel.

"Lara," I say again, shock bleeding into laughter. Good thing we're the only apartments on this floor, else we'd have a third person hammering on my door. She shoves harder on my shoulders, jaw clenched with effort.

Nope. Not gonna kneel that easily.

"Just showing you what I've learned," she says, breathless, and then it's *my* turn to take control.

"Shouldn't start a fight you can't finish, sweetheart." I explode forward, lifting her in a fireman's hold. And my shy, nerdy neighbor pounds on my back, whooping with laughter, her legs kicking as I carry her to the center of the living room.

The coffee table judders along the floor as I push it out of the way with my foot. Oops.

"Shh," I hiss as I place Lara, bright-eyed and flushed, on the rug. "You need to submit to this humiliating defeat quietly." Sounds are muffled in this building, but they're not *that* muffled. "Now show me your stance."

Lara rolls her eyes, but raises both fists; she rocks onto the balls of her feet, her white pajamas all twisted around her body.

I slap one fist down. She prods my stomach before raising it again.

I lunge for her shoulders.

She dances back.

"Slippery little thing, aren't you?" We circle each other in the lamplight, eyes glowing bright, cheeks flushed. Her pulse taps frantically under her jaw, and I've never seen her look so feral.

So beautiful.

After earlier, I thought… but she's here, isn't she? And I won't push her further than she wants to go. I'll never do that. If all Lara wants tonight is a jokey wrestle and a kiss on the cheek, that's what I'll give her.

"You're not trying very hard," she murmurs, and we're both quieter now that we've remembered the other people in this building. The loudest sound in the room is our heavy breaths and the soft creak of our footsteps. "Why are you holding back?"

"Earlier." I feint toward my neighbor; she dodges easily. "I freaked you out."

Lara's mouth twists. "I freaked *myself* out. But… I'm feeling braver now."

"Because the break-in crew was caught?"

Her smile is so secretive. "Sure. Let's say that."

Ha. I've got that tickly feeling, you know the one? This joke is definitely on me. And when I lunge for her this time, I show no mercy.

Her pajamas are silky, sliding against her skin, but I bear her down to the floor before she even gets a chance to react. Straddling Lara's hips, I pin her wrists on either side of her head.

"Oof," she says. "You weigh a ton, Dawson."

I lighten up a tiny bit. Don't want to squish the girl of my dreams.

"Fight back," I tell her, squeezing her wrists. "Escape this hold. Come on, princess. Show me how it's done."

"You're unbearable," she wheezes, bucking and writhing against the rug. I stay rooted, careful to pin her with my weight—but not to crush her.

"What did Sarge even teach you?" I ask, all mock sadness, though I'm having way too much fun watching her wriggle beneath me. "This is self defense 101—"

I cut off as Lara shoves her hips up, knocking me off balance. Her hands slip free, and then she's tipping us, rolling us over.

I land with a grunt, way too pleased to feel my neighbor's soft curves land on top of my body. Lara pins me the same way I pinned her, pressing my wrists down against the rug. How are her braids still immaculate? I feel rumpled to shit.

"Fight back," she says, her chest rising and falling with each breath. "Come on, fight back."

I wriggle to get comfy, feeling the warmth of her seep through my sweatpants. "No, thank you."

"Dawson—"

"Shh. I'm busy."

Lara snorts, and then I feel the vibrations of her giggles *everywhere.*

"You're awful."

I slip my hands free and spread them over her bare thighs, rubbing my thumbs back and forth. So soft. So squeezable. "So I've been told."

Her breath catches, and then it's like the air changes in the room. We go from warmth and teasing and laughter to something else.

Something heavier. Something dark and delicious.

When Lara leans down, I'm already pushing up on my elbows to meet her. We kiss urgently, mouths clashing together, no finesse—just hunger. And though I thought I was already hot and bothered, I was wrong, because *this* is heat, scorching my whole body from the inside.

She moans quietly, tilting her head to kiss me again. I slide my tongue against hers and she nips my lip hard enough to sting.

Fuck. My beard rasps beneath her fingernails; the room spins and my chest throbs.

Love her so much. Wanted this for so long. And now I can't think, can't speak, can't do anything except kiss her deeper, my hips rocking up to rub against her body.

I break away in a daze, gritting out an apology, but Lara hushes me and grinds our bodies together even harder.

"Yeah?" I ask, hardly daring to believe my luck. Her and me? How the fuck will I ever be worthy?

"Yes," Lara says, pushing my t-shirt up to bare my torso. She rakes me with her nails, and my head tips back on a groan.

"Up here." I tap on my chest, collapsing back against the rug with zero grace. My head smacks against the floor, but I don't care. Don't care. My stomach's sucking in with each breath, my lungs working overtime, and all I can think of is getting my mouth on those prissy little shorts. "Sit on my face, sweetheart."

"Oh." Lara blinks down at me, shocked at the very suggestion. And Christ, if I don't find that even more irresistible.

Just want to rumple her up. Want to shock her and please her, and fog up those prim reading glasses she wears sometimes.

Should I ask her to fetch them now?

No, jackass. Focus.

"Is that—how will you breathe?"

I tap my throat. "Secret gills. Come on, Lara, smother me to death. You know you've always wanted to."

"Not like *this*," she mutters, but she's crawling along my body, so careful where she puts her hands and knees.

Outside the dark window, the city skyline pulses with light. The faint sounds of traffic float up from the street, even at this late hour, and headlights snake between buildings.

The floorboards groan softly as one knee settles beside my head, then the other. Lara sits her ass back on my chest, fingers plucking at the t-shirt bunched up around my neck.

"I'm worried I might hurt you."

I'm already shaking my head. "Not gonna happen, but if you do I'll tap your leg. Okay?"

She chews her bottom lip, and there's something more. I wait, aiming for patience, even though my mouth's already watering with her so close.

Lara sucks in a deep breath. Her shoulders brace, and she tells the opposite wall: "I'm worried I might... smell. Or taste weird. I showered before bed, but I... still. I'm worried."

Ah, hell. My chest aches with how badly I want to make this woman feel good. I'd give anything to see her confidence bloom.

"Lara? Look at me." It takes a few breaths, but she finally

looks down. Meets my eye, and she's so vulnerable, it steals all my air. "I promise you that those are baseless fears," I tell her. And she opens her mouth to argue, but I'm already pushing on: "But if not, we'll take another shower together, okay? I'll be honest with you, I swear. Scout's honor."

Her lips press together. She fidgets with my t-shirt. "Promise?" she says at last.

"Promise."

Another beat. Then: "Okay."

We cooled off a little while we talked, and now I stroke my palms up and down her thighs, trying to coax some heat back between us. And it takes a few seconds, but then Lara sighs and squirms, her body rocking against mine, and yeah... yeah.

My thumbs creep closer together, swooping across her inner thighs. Closer, closer...

"Oh," Lara murmurs, her eyes drifting closed as I rub her gently though her shorts. "Oh—*oh*. Okay. That feels nice."

She's gripping my shoulders now, squeezing me tight and releasing, like a kitten pedaling with tiny claws. Her hips rock against my touch, chasing my feather-light thumbs.

"Stop teasing," Lara begs at last, her head tipping back.

"Come closer, then. You know what to do."

She curses quietly—and have I ever heard my prim neighbor curse before? God, I love this—but shifts obediently closer, pushing up to kneel with her thighs parting a few inches above my face. She's kept her pajama shorts on, but that's okay. The fabric's thin, and they're loose enough to tug to the side.

"I'm going to make you feel so good, I promise." My hands cup the backs of her thighs, kneading and stroking. "God, just look at you. So perfect, Lara."

She lowers down with my urging, thighs trembling on either

side of my face. They're thick and soft and butter-smooth, and Christ, this is it. This is how I want to go.

"Don't be shy," I say as she gets closer. "Sit, don't hover. Remember how much you've hated me, Lara? All those times you wanted to smother me? This is your chance, baby. Do it for your past self. Do it for her."

She snorts, though it sounds kind of strangled. Her weight settles over me and I breathe in deeply, letting out a pleased grunt.

"I never hated you," she says, but I'm barely listening. She's damp already, slick and seeping through her shorts, and she's so sweet and salty and musky and perfect.

Fuck, I want to rub this all over my body. Want her scent on my bed sheets.

"Is it, um." Lara gasps as I lick her through the shorts, sucking and lapping through the fabric. My jaw already aches from the weight of her, but I don't care. "Is it okay?"

Better than okay, I want to say, but my mouth is too busy. I settle on a loud groan, rubbing my whole face between her thighs, squeezing her ass with both hands.

Lara's laugh is breathless. Her fingers play in my hair, tugging and twisting the strands, and I tease her shorts to one side with my tongue. Take my first full lick of her bare slit.

"Oh!" Lara bucks forward, then babbles an apology.

Don't care. This would be one broken nose I'd treasure. And I lick and suck and nibble her, jaw clicking, tongue aching, snatching my oxygen through quick inhales as her body shifts.

"D-Dawson."

Yeah, I like how she says my name when she's like this. All quavery and broken. I squeeze her ass harder, plunging my tongue as deep as it will go, and she lets out a breathless wail.

We rock together, my face buried between her trembling thighs. Sweat pools in the small of my back, and I'm downright smothered, but I don't care. Never want to stop. I drag it out as long as I can, chasing her higher, then settling her down again, higher, then down, until Lara yanks on my hair.

"Dawson! *God.*"

Okay, okay. I change tact, because the frustration in her voice was almost painful, and I guess I need to breathe or whatever. Wedging her thighs a little wider, I go *at* her, lapping at her nub, until—

"Shit!" Lara says, and it sounds like all the air's gone from her chest. "Shit!"

She freezes up, twitching and groaning. It's like a huge wave, crashing over her whole body from top to toe, rattling her hard enough that her shudders shake me too. Clinging on for my goddamn life, I lick her through it, until Lara bats me away and collapses to one side, and I'm left with a slick beard and a goofy grin on my face.

I suck down air, reaching out to grasp the nearest part of her. A smooth, brown ankle. Her racing pulse taps against my fingertip.

"Wow," Lara says at last. She sounds as dazed as I feel, and we're both sprawled on the rug like two puppets with our strings cut. So good. And I should move, I *want* to move, but this moment is too perfect and my limbs are heavy as lead.

Come on, asshole. Look alive.

One more minute passes, then Lara tilts her head and gazes at me. Cracks a smile. Then she shuffles around, slinging a thigh over my waist again. "Okay, I'm back in the room. Where were we?"

Lara

If there's one thing I've learned over the last few weeks, it's that bravery is a choice. I don't have to be paralyzed with fear when there are break-ins on my block, or when my crush on my maddening neighbor leaves me tongue-tied.

I can take self defense classes. Can take measures to feel safer.

And I can go after what I want.

Sure, there are still risks in life, but at least I'm *doing* it, you know? Living fully. Being brave.

And right now, Brave Lara wants to get as close to this man as humanly possible. What we just did—feeling his hungry mouth between my thighs—that felt insanely good, but it's not enough. There's still a restlessness coursing through my body.

"We can stop," Dawson rasps, his chest still working hard to bring air into his lungs. Jeez, did he really get that out of breath? Why the hell didn't he tap me to kneel up? If he ever lets me smother him to death by mistake, I'll kill him. "We don't need to rush, sweetheart."

I know we don't *need* to. But maybe I want to, you know? I'm twenty four years old, damn it. I've had plenty of run up.

And lord knows I've craved this man for a long time.

"I want to keep going." Rocking our bodies together, I bite my lip and stare down. "Do you want to keep going?"

Dawson makes a choked noise. Kind of like: "Chyuh."

"Words, please."

He scoffs, but he's gripping my thighs again. Stroking and kneading. "*Yes*, Lara. I obviously want to keep going. Can't you feel me digging into your ass cheek?"

"I want to be sure," I tell him primly, reaching back to tease his waistband down. It sticks for a second on his rigid length, but Dawson lifts his hips and helps me out. He springs free, and he's so hot and firm in my hand.

The skin is so silky, sliding up and down his shaft. Dawson's jaw clenches, and he groans between his teeth as I work him. The angle's kind of weird, my arm twisted behind my back, but I don't think he minds.

Does he know I've never done this before? Would it put him off if I confessed? The same anxieties from earlier crowd in, buzzing around my head like hornets, but I breathe through them and keep stroking.

If he's happy, I'm happy. No one's great on their first time, right? And Dawson's never been a judgmental person, even when others have side-eyed me for my manners or choices. He's always grinned at me, all soppy and fond.

It used to aggravate me—like I was the butt of his joke, or something.

But now I know better.

"Go gently," Dawson murmurs, proving once again that he knows me inside out; that he can read me like no one else can.

He's still stroking my thighs, and it's so soothing. "It can hurt the first time, so just go easy, okay? And if you don't like it, we'll stop."

I should have known he'd be sweet about this. So many times, I should have given him the benefit of the doubt.

Going forward, I am *all* about Team Dawson. I tug my ruined pajama shorts to one side and notch him at my entrance.

"Jesus," he grits out when I'm halfway down. I nod, muscles shivering, too dazed by these sensations to speak. Because he's so *thick*. So hard. Pressing inside me, dragging over all these nerve endings I didn't even know I had, lighting me up from the inside out.

I bite my lip hard, working myself down another inch. Dawson's frowning at the ceiling, and his lips are moving.

"What are you saying?" I ask, once I get my tongue to work.

Dawson's mouth curls up, but he keeps staring at the ceiling. "I'm trying not to disgrace myself, Lara. Distracting myself."

"With?"

He has the grace to look embarrassed, at least. "Going through the stunt routine for a movie next week."

"Dawson!"

"Sorry, sorry." Finally, he looks at me, his eyes crinkling with humor. "If it helps, it didn't work. I can't focus on anything except how goddamn perfect you feel around my cock. So tight and slick," he thrusts up gently, sinking another inch, "so *warm*. Like sinking into a hot bath."

"Don't be a weirdo," I tell him, but secretly I'm thrilled. I really feel that good to him? He likes this as much as I do?

"I'm serious." My neighbor thrusts up again, bouncing me gently in his lap, and we both groan as we seal fully together. He's all the way in. Not a single obstacle between us.

"This, Lara, is the best thing I've ever felt. You know what you've done, letting me feel this? You know how much I'm gonna hound you now, begging for another taste? Another feel? Another chance at heaven?"

He's so chatty, his mouth running away from him as his gaze roves up and down my body. I lean back and flick my shirt buttons open, one by one, slowly baring my stomach and my heavy breasts with their hard, brown nipples.

Dawson stares like he never wants to blink again.

"Yeah, you've done it now. I can't give this up. No way, no how. I'm gonna need this morning, noon and night, Lara, but don't worry—I'll make it good for you too. Make you moan so loud that the laundry ladies complain."

"Shut up," I whisper, choking back laughter, but I don't mean it. I love this. Love *him*.

Love how far gone he is for me, ranting like he's lost control of his tongue, declaring that I'm his and no one else's and he'll never give me up. That he's gonna keep me forever and worship the ground I walk on.

As if that's any kind of threat. More like my wildest dreams come true.

"I'm still me," I warn him, rising and falling over his lap, dragging my body up and down his length. We're moving faster now, faster and harder, floorboards creaking beneath our joined weight. "Don't forget who you're talking to. I'm still your prissy neighbor who thinks writing a college paper is a good time; I'm still a giant nerd. I'll be in bed by 10pm most nights."

Dawson beams, rocking his head back and forth, his eyes falling closed like he's in pure bliss. "Stop it, Lara. Stop promising me the world. I can't fucking take it."

116

His hand snakes between us, thumb dipping inside my shorts to rub circles on my clit. My breath stutters, and I grind down harder.

Every nerve ending in my body sizzles with life. If you could see them, I'd be lit up like that city skyline: thousands upon thousands of glowing lights.

"I love you." Dawson catches my hand; tangles our fingers together. I grip on too, clinging on for dear life as I ride. "Let's not go backwards, okay? No more fighting unless it's play wrestling. Agreed?"

My heart is so full. I squeeze his fingers. "Agreed."

And this time, when I come, it's deeper. Richer. The tingles start somewhere deep inside my body, then reverberate outward, sweeping away every last thought in my brain. I feel it in my toes and in my fingertips. My temples pound.

And when I slump over Dawson's chest, breathing raggedly, he thrusts up into me twice more—then stills. His shaft swells and spills inside me, painting me in hot spurts.

"Ew," I mumble against his collarbone, though when I get past the stickiness... I kind of like it.

The primalness of it. The feeling of being claimed. The cosmic bargain we're sealing together.

"Don't worry." Dawson taps my thigh with a clumsy hand. His voice is thick with exhaustion, and his whole body is boneless beneath me. Slumped and sated. "I'll buy you new pajamas, princess."

I hide my smile against his beard. "Shut up."

117

Dawson

One year later

"Oh my god," Lara says, bouncing on the sidewalk by my elbow. She's practically fizzing with excitement, clinging to my free hand as I fiddle with the front door to The Corner. "Are you sure this is okay? I can't believe we're doing this."

So fucking cute. "Relax, Jax gave me spare keys to this place years ago. It's hardly a break in."

"But you did tell him we were coming here after hours, right? You let him know?"

I shrug, nudging the door open at last. It swings into an empty, shadowed gym. Our footsteps echo as we shuffle inside, closing the door to the late night street behind us. The rumble of cars fades away, and our breathing sounds louder in here.

"Nope, I didn't tell him. Why don't you debate the ethics of that at your fancy college on Monday?"

She snorts, punching my arm in the darkness. Lara knows

I'm only teasing: I couldn't be prouder of my brainbox wife if I tried.

"You are such a bad influence."

"Too late to escape me now." I squeeze her hand, leading her across the empty floor. It looks even bigger than usual in the gloom, completely clear without sparring partners or mats. Like a dark, shadowy ocean. "Just don't steal anything or write on the walls. Jax never needs to know we were here."

"But—"

"Princess, if you don't get on board, I'm gonna fuck you right on the desk in his office. Is that what you want, huh?"

Her giggles float through the cavernous space, and finally she hisses, "Don't you dare."

Well, we're not here to fight, that's for sure. With her bump just starting to show, my wife's in no condition to spar. But our apartment building really echoes, and sometimes, you know...

We like to get loud. Sue us.

A light flicks on across the gym. One of the back rooms, with a window open to the main gym floor.

"Get behind me," I mutter, my whole body rigid and all humor gone. Lara slips behind my back, and I stare into the lit up room, my heart hammering.

What have I brought her into? What the hell is happening?

Who else is here in the middle of the night?

No signs of a break in. My brain whirs extra fast, clicking through the options, adrenaline giving me clarity. Maybe Jax and Casey had the same idea...?

A figure shuffles into view, small and slight. A young woman. She turns and hops up onto a table, and I frown across the huge gym, trying to stare into the room but not willing to go any closer.

The glow of electric light burns my eyes. Who the hell is she?

Then another figure steps into view, broad and looming and auburn-haired. *Sarge.* The Scot moves close to the strange woman, ducking his head as they chat. I've *never* seen him smile at someone like that.

"This motherfucker," I breathe, and a finger prods me in the ribs.

"Who is it?" Lara hisses.

"Sarge. Look."

She steps around me, then makes a small sound of surprise. Lara's spent plenty of time around my buddies over the last year, but I know she still finds Sarge kinda eerie. He's just so *big* and brooding and he never, ever smiles.

"Who's that with him?"

"No idea." I reach down and find her hand in the darkness. "Come on. Let's leave Sarge to it. If he finds out that we've witnessed him experiencing an emotion, he'll kill us both and hide our bodies under the mat pile."

"But what about… you know…" Lara drags her feet as I lead her back to the door, sighing tragically as I let us both out onto the street. "We had *plans*, Dawson."

"Oh yeah?" I spin the key in the lock, my gut heavy with disappointment too. "You want Sarge to hear those plans?"

Nope. She shakes her head fast, and neither do I. But then I brighten, tugging her down the sidewalk, because for once, *I'm* the one with a brainwave.

"Tell me, princess: how do you feel about being gagged?"

Lara scoffs loudly, but walks faster. Her fingers cling tighter to mine, and oh yeah, she's into it. So am I. "I think you're a caveman, Reynolds."

"And I think you love it." My wife can't hide anything from

me. She's so damn cute. So eager and sweet and sexy.

Yeah, we'll figure something out. We'll problem solve our gnarly hookup.

We're a good team. We always do.

III

Going Rogue

Description

~~~
❧⁂❧
~~~

He's a grumpy giant with swollen knuckles and a broken nose.

But he's secretly gentle with me.

I didn't come to the boxing gym to fight. Are you kidding? With these shrimp arms? I'd be a stain on the floor in ten seconds flat.

Nope, I came to find someone special. Someone rough and brawny, who I could use as a model for my comic book art. The world's most unlikely muse.

And I found him, alright. Sarge talks in grunts and towers over grown men. He's mean-looking and scary. He's *perfect*.

I'm shocked when he agrees.

And I'm *extra* shocked by my sudden crush.

Because once I look at the giant properly... I can't look away.

Phoebe

The boxing gym smells like sweat, blood, and cleaning spray. The windows are thrown open to the street, coaxing in a fresh fall breeze, but this huge room's still several degrees warmer than outside. Sunshine falls in big, golden shafts across the floor, and the fighters have dragged their mats away from the extra heat, grappling in the shade.

Thump. Smack. Grunt.

Music hums in the background, floating from the speakers in the rafters. The towering walls are white.

My backpack is weighed down with art supplies, the straps digging into my thin shoulders, and I bump it higher as I walk. Blowing my dark bangs off my sweaty forehead, I peer at every fighter I pass.

Nope.

No.

No way.

Too smiley.

Too pretty. How'd you keep a nose that straight when you're

doing *this* on a Wednesday night? I wrinkle my own, staring openly at each person I walk past, sizing up their features and watching how they move.

Coming to a boxing gym was a genius level brain wave, no doubt about it. There's bound to be someone here I can draw.

An extra loud thump echoes across the room, followed by whoops and hollers. I glance over, changing direction so I'm headed toward all the fuss, my heavy boots clomping against the floor.

People stare as I pass, but I don't care. I'm used to that. I know I'm weird looking, and besides, I clearly don't belong in this gym. All that matters is finding a muse—I'm not here to make friends.

I remind myself that as I go, over and over, trying to ignore the knot in my stomach.

Sometimes, I wish I could blend in at least a tiny bit. It was the same back in high school, and now in the art supply shop where I work to pay the bills.

It's like everyone else *gets* it. You know? Like they all have a secret manual of the right things to say and the correct moments to laugh and smile. Like they took a class together that never made it onto my timetable. How to make a friend 101.

Whatever. If I had a social life growing up, I'd have spent way less time drawing, and I'd be years behind where I am now. So... yay for me?

There's a crowd gathered around a boxing ring—a proper raised one with ropes. Everyone presses close, hissing and oohing, flinching together when an especially brutal hit lands, and I hide a smirk as I elbow my way through the sweaty bodies.

Hey, these people may be MMA legends or whatever, and

they may stand head and shoulders above me, but I have very pointy elbows and steel toe-capped boots. We all have our weapons.

"Come on," a man bellows in the ring as I shove my way to a gap at the front. My chin's level with the middle rope. "Put your backs into it!"

There's a Scottish burr to his deep voice, and it's so powerful, it's like the walls quake. I swear, the lights overhead flicker in their wire cages.

He beats his bare chest, slick with sweat and pocked with scars. Two other men square off with him, both dressed in the gym's uniform of black t-shirts and sweatpants. They sag where they stand, clearly exhausted.

Oh, wow. Chewing on my bottom lip, I press closer to the ring until the rough rope scrapes my chin.

It's two against one, and this guy makes it look easy. They're both breathing hard, raised fists drooping, but he just looks pissed off and bored. What must that kind of strength feel like?

I'd be terrible with power like that, for the record. I'd throw my big, muscly weight around and do whatever I liked; be a real tyrant. So it's probably a good thing that I'm barely five feet tall with reedy limbs.

"Another!" the giant Scot calls, like he's ordering a beer. A third man launches into the ring, ducking between the ropes as the crowd smacks his back and yells encouragement. This guy's blond and bearded, dressed in all black too, and in most rooms he'd probably look like a viking—but not here.

Here, he's squaring off against an angry Scottish mountain. Three against one, and I still don't like their chances.

I swallow hard as the bare-chested man wipes his face on a thick, corded forearm, then waves them all forward.

He's got coppery red hair, pushed back from his forehead and curling round his ears. In his late thirties, maybe, and weathered. His jaw is square, and tattoos ripple over his chest and arms as he fights.

Yeesh. I shift my weight, a strange heaviness settling low in my belly. I could *definitely* draw this guy. For hours and hours, never getting bored.

Each punch he throws is like an anvil whistling through the air. He's light on his feet, agile, but he looks big enough to snap a barge in two.

The new blond fighter spins on his heel; his kick lands hard on the mountain's lower back. The Scot grins and grips the man's ankle, then tosses him overhead like a rag doll.

On and on they fight, the crowd groaning and stamping their feet. The whole gym is here now, whipped into a frenzy, their own mats abandoned on the huge floor. The Scot never hurts anyone too badly—never knocks them out or breaks a bone—but they're all struggling now, weaving on their feet.

It's nice of this man to put on a show. He's made my treasure hunt super easy, because it's *him.*

I want him. If I don't draw this man, I'll go mad.

My fingers itch to grip a pencil.

"Sarge," someone calls from a faraway door. Two dark-haired men lounge in what looks like an office entrance, the bearded one grinning and shaking his head. They're in the regulation black sweatpants too, but their white t-shirts set them apart from the crowd.

"Wrap this up, will you?" the first one says, his calm voice carrying across the space. "Casey's bringing the baby soon. I don't want her first word to be 'bloodbath.'"

The Scot grunts, scowling at his three opponents with

renewed focus.

One—the most exhausted—raises his palms, backing up. "I'm out. Sorry, Sarge."

Sarge looks disappointed for a split second, but he nods. And he's all set to finish against the other two, but they're backing up as well, taking the easy way out.

"Good fight, man."

"Yeah, you wiped the floor with us."

Ugh. I press my chin against the rope, glowering at the battered men as they duck out of the ring, steadied by a dozen hands. They're greeted like heroes, but they didn't even finish!

God, the least they could do is let him lay them out. They should be honored that a man like that fought them at all. I shake my head, teeth grinding with frustration, and when I glance up at the ring—

Electric blue eyes stare into mine. The Scot watches me, noting my irritation, and for the tiniest moment, his mouth twitches.

Then he's turning away, muscles flexing in his broad back as he ducks out of the ring. His fingers shake slightly where he holds the rope up, his knuckles bleeding and swollen.

The crowd welcomes him down with cheers—but they scatter back, giving him a wide berth. No one steadies the victor.

I suck on my teeth, watching Sarge walk away. He heads toward the changing rooms, and he's so obviously alone in this crowd.

Like me.

Sarge

Is there anything worse than a fight with no finish? It's worse than any blue balls, I swear. Like someone taking hours to slow roast a meal, the scents wafting through the kitchen—then tipping it straight into the trash. Like reading a book to the last chapter, then slamming it shut and never knowing how it ends.

Jesus.

Scrubbing a hand towel over my face, I cross the gym floor, trying and failing to push away the violence thrumming in my veins. My stomach's tense. If we could've just *finished*…

But we didn't, and now I'm wound tighter than a ratchet strap. My chest is puffed up and tight, and tendons stand out in my throat. My hands shake, and my temples pound.

It'll take hours to burn this energy off. No real point showering, since I'll need to run the river path, or beat a punching bag until it bursts. But maybe a blast of icy water will take the edge off.

I don't notice I'm being followed until I'm halfway to the

changing room double doors. Then it nudges at my brain: the *clomp, clomp, clomp* of heavy boots right behind me.

I spin around, annoyed, because as a fighter I should have better instincts than this, but no one ever follows me. No one wants to get too near me, period.

The young woman stumbles to a halt, clutching her backpack straps. Christ, she's tiny. I could balance her on the palm of my hand. Even in that baggy plaid shirt, she's small.

"What?" I snap, glowering even harder when she flinches. If she's so damn scared of me, why follow me like a stray cat?

The woman says something, her lips moving, but I don't catch the words in the loud gym. Everyone else has gone back to their own fights, and the music sounds louder now without the roar of the crowd.

"Speak up," I say, and I shouldn't be such a dick, but that unfinished fight is twisting my guts. Need that ice-cold shower, stat. I'm not fit for company right now.

"I want to draw you," the woman mumbles, jiggling her backpack like that illustrates her point. "For my graphic novel."

Uh. What?

Shit. Who'd ever want to draw *me*?

My scornful bark of laughter makes her flinch even worse than before. Her eyes dart to the side then back, and she's trembling, but she stands her ground.

Choppy black hair, with heavy bangs over wide, brown eyes. Olive skin and a pointy chin. This girl's delicate, easily half the size of those guys from the ring, but she's facing me down with twice as much courage. Her chin raises.

"I'll pay you," she says, clearer now. "Artists pay their models. And you'd keep your clothes on—"

"I should fucking hope so," I splutter, my ruddy cheeks

getting warmer.

"—in fact, I'd like to draw you mid-fight. So you wouldn't need to do anything different; you wouldn't even know I was there at all."

I doubt that somehow. Even back there in the ring, I noticed her right away, wriggling her way to the front then scowling at the fight like she was hungry for blood. It was hard to focus with her watching, and we'd never even spoken.

Besides, I'm not the kind of man anyone draws. I'm never in photos, and when people look at me twice, it's with fear, not interest.

This can't happen.

"Not interested."

I walk away without another word, scrubbing the towel over my face again. I'm not that sweaty anymore—just want to feel the fabric rasp over my skin, rough and grounding.

Her boots clomp along behind me. Is she gonna follow me all the way into the showers?

"You don't understand," she says, and she's puffing to keep up with my long strides. "I *need* to draw you. Need to."

And I needed to flatten those three guys in the ring. We don't always get what we want, do we?

"I said I'm not interested." My palms smack against the changing room doors, the air turning cooler through here, and I'm relieved to enter alone.

* * *

"The thing is," the young woman says as I step back out into the gym, freshly showered and dressed in clean clothes, "you wouldn't have to change your routine or do anything different.

I'm not asking for all that much."

She's still here? She waited?

The woman falls back into step beside me as I head for Jax's office, and I clench my jaw to keep from snapping at her.

Not asking that much? She wants to draw my face and body, commit all of *this* to paper, and she's not asking that much?

I know what I am: a brute. In body and soul. I've come to terms with that, and I make it work in my favor. I'm famous on the bare-knuckle circuit, and though barely anyone gets close enough to be a friend... well, no one causes me any trouble, either.

Doesn't mean I want some pretty little thing to rub it in. If I could choose my appearance, I sure wouldn't choose this.

"No."

"*Please* reconsider. You'd be perfect for my story."

I bet I would. Bet she'd love to draw her hero beating the crap out of me. But she's out of breath, hurrying to keep up with my long steps, and despite myself, I slow down. She'll hurt herself if she kicks her own ankle with those boots.

"Maybe we could do some kind of trade—"

"And what," I growl, slamming to a halt and turning on her, "could you possibly have to offer me?"

She stutters, her neck craning, and I'm so much bigger, rougher, meaner. A monster, with my shoulders stretching my own clothes. This young woman's like a scruffy little blackbird hopping around my feet, pecking at crumbs.

"Well, you don't have to be a dick about it," she says bluntly.

And Christ, no one talks to me like that. No one calls me out when I'm being rude. And though shame tickles the back of my neck... I'm pleased.

When was the last time somebody treated me like this? Like

135

a regular man? Besides Jax and Dawson and their wives, I don't remember.

Feels good.

So she wants to put my ugly mug in her graphic novel. Who cares? Maybe it's worth it if this girl will treat me like a normal human being.

"Alright." I give a curt nod. "I'll do it. Come back tomorrow."

She blinks at my rapid one-eighty, then scowls beneath those messy bangs like I'm trying to trick her somehow. And god, I love that she's not scared of me at all. She looks ready to kick me in the shin if I step out of line. Such a feisty little scrap.

"Just like that?" The doubt's clear in her voice. "Will you really come? Are you setting me up?"

The thought did cross my mind, but... nope.

"I'll be here. Fully clothed," I add, and I don't smile, but my cheeks ache like maybe they want to.

Her mouth twists, and here we are: little and large. Pointedly *not* smiling at each other, but standing closer than we were a minute ago. We've reached some kind of truce.

"Tomorrow," she says slowly. "The same time?"

"The same time."

"Maybe I'll see you actually finish a fight." She smirks, and she's got that hungry look again. The bloodthirstiness.

For both our sakes, I hope so.

Phoebe

I rush across town straight from my shift in the art supply store, bag thumping against my back as I jog through the crowded streets. My boots thud against the sidewalk, and a steady stream of people flow past. Thick socks cushion my toes from the steel caps, but I'm dressed in black ripped jeans and a moss green sweater—not exactly a prime running outfit.

Didn't have time to change. No time to do anything except grab my bag, lock up, and run through the city beneath the lavender sky.

Now I'm sticky. Sweat slides down my spine and gathers between my tiny boobs. As I wait for the lights at a pedestrian crossing to change, I risk a sniff of my armpit, then groan.

Maybe The Corner will smell too strongly of other people's sweat for Sarge to notice I reek. A whole shift of humping boxes in the store room, and now this?

Fingers crossed. Don't want him repulsed, though I'm not sure why the thought bothers me so much.

The lights change, and I suck in a deep breath before I set off again, bag jostling. Crap, I am not built for cardio. The only thing reedier than my muscles is my lungs. But it's the only way to get across town in time, and I'm worried that if I'm even ten minutes late, the angry Scottish mountain will change his mind.

I *need* to draw him. Couldn't sleep last night, I was thinking about it so much. The way his muscles bunched and flexed as he moved in that ring, shiny with sweat... the way he towered over everyone, so strong and proud...

If I don't draw this man, I will lose my mind.

Trees line this block, their trunks hemmed in by black railings, and locked bicycles slump against their roots. The leaves above have just begun to turn red and gold, drying and curling on the branch, and the fallen ones skitter between the crowd's feet.

Crunch.

Nothing better than stomping on a dried leaf.

By the time I reach The Corner, I've mentally won the Olympic gold and retired from running after a glorious career. I swipe my sleeve across my forehead, staring up at the sign and willing my breaths to slow.

Clean black and white design. A good font. Nice.

Someone exits the gym, flashing me an odd look as they step past, and the sounds inside are louder until the door swings closed.

I check my phone; sniff my sweater again and wince. Pluck the fabric away from my skin and waft it, trying to cool down. Come up with a million excuses not to go inside.

And... what the hell am I doing? Am I gonna waste the whole night out here? I'm sticky and gross from running over here—it is what it is. Not about to change.

Stifling a groan at my own cowardice, I grit my teeth and push through the doors.

* * *

"Like this?" Sarge calls from ten feet away, squaring off against a man called Jax. This guy's dark haired with a stubbled jaw, broad and well built, and though there's only one of him, he's faring way better than the three guys from yesterday.

Jax turns to look at me too, but he doesn't give a shit about my drawings. He's staring between me and Sarge, his expression rapt.

"Yeah," I call back, smudging Sarge's bicep with my thumb. He's got a black t-shirt on today, sadly, but I'm trying to hide my disappointment. That *chest*. I'm haunted by that chest. "Don't worry about it too much. Just carry on like normal, and I'll move if I need to."

It's not like I'm super attached to this stack of mats. Every time someone wants one, I have to hop down and stop drawing for a minute before I can resettle. At least I can sit cross legged, with my sketchbook balanced across my knees.

Sarge grunts and turns back to the fight. He waits until his opponent is focused too, then swings a punch, forcing Jax back.

They circle each other, jabbing and ducking. Lunging and kicking. This fight's way harder for Sarge, I can tell—and I can also tell he loves it. He's exhilarated, his teeth gleaming as he grins, and I switch to drawing a close up of that battered face.

Battered but kinda beautiful. My tummy swoops, and I outline his nose.

When I arrived here tonight, I was so sure that he'd bail. That—if he even showed at all—he'd tell me our deal was off,

139

and to get gone. But Sarge walked right over to me as soon as I stepped through the doors, and it's funny... it's like he was *shy*.

Can a giant, rough mountain of a man be shy? Doesn't that break the rules of nature?

But here he is, shooting me cautious looks whenever he gets a chance, his cheeks flushing darker like he's self conscious. Now and then, he tugs at the hem of his black t-shirt, like he's worried it's gotten twisted.

He doesn't need to worry about that. I mean, I wish it'd come off altogether, but more to the point—I'm gonna make him look *good*. Not by changing anything, but with pure honesty.

There's no other way to draw this man. His face and body, the way he moves... it calls for reverence.

"Time," Jax says, making a T shape with his hands. "I need to finish up in the office before Case gets here."

"Sure." Sarge nods, but I can feel the tension rolling off him as yet another fight ends early. He scrubs at his jaw, then wanders over to my perch. The mats hiss as he sits heavily by my side. "Jesus Christ, what I'd give to finish a fight," he mutters.

I bet. Must be so frustrating. Like starting a bunch of sketches that you never get to finish.

"Look." Nudging him in the ribs, I tilt my sketchbook. "This will distract you. What do you think so far?"

Sarge stares at the rough outlines; the hurried shading. He tilts his head, and his frown deepens.

Huh.

Someone hollers across the gym, and sneakers squeak against the floor. My stomach is so tense, like I've done a hundred sit-ups. Doesn't he like them? I know these drawings are rough, but I'm *good*, okay? It's the one thing I've got going for me. Doesn't he see that?

"I'll clean them up later," I say, defensiveness snapping through my words. "These aren't finished yet."

Sarge says nothing. He's still brooding, leaning down to see my sketchbook better, the mats creaking. His body is so warm by my side, and his sweat smells fresh.

Ugh. Why'd I even show him at all? That wasn't part of our agreement. I could've drawn stick figures for all he knew.

Didn't know how badly I wanted his approval until now.

"You've photoshopped me," Sarge says at last. He sounds disappointed, and I hate that. Hate everything about this. Because I wanted him to like them, okay? Wanted him to admire my skills, the way I admire his.

I'm such an idiot.

"Photoshop is a computer program," I tell him in a flat voice.

"You know what I mean. You've doctored me. Made me look better than I am."

"No I haven't." I snatch up the sketchbook, tilting this way and that, trying to see what he means. My sketches are rough, sure, but I've never tried to pretty-up my subjects. Why the hell would I do such a boring thing? The flaws are the best bit! "This is accurate! See, there's your broken nose, and those are the scars on your arms, and there are the lines by your eyes—"

"Alright, alright. I get the picture."

The fighter leans back and folds his arms over his chest. He stares at the drawings, and he still looks puzzled. On the pages, the sketched Sarge lunges in one pose; stands tall in another; kicks out a powerful leg. The close up of his face grins wide, exhilarated by the challenge.

There's hero worship in every pencil stroke, and it's so raw that I want to scrunch the whole page into a ball.

"Well, I'm done here." I slam the sketchbook shut. My boots

catch on the mats as I wriggle my legs straight. I've been sitting cross-legged for too long, and pins and needles prickle up my calves. "Got plenty to go on. Hope you get to finish a fight soon."

"Phoebe."

Earlier tonight, when he said my name for the first time in that deep, Scottish burr, I shivered all over. Now it just makes my stomach do this sad little flip. My feet thump against the floor, and I snatch up my backpack. Stuff my sketchbook and pencils away.

"*Phoebe*. Why are you running away?"

I'm not running. Who's running? But I've got enough material for my graphic novel, and there's no point lingering, is there? Got places to be. Pillows to punch.

Sarge pinches the sleeve of my sweater. "I'm not letting you go until you tell me what's wrong."

"That's kidnapping," I say, trying to shrug him off. He won't let go. "I'll scream for help."

"No, you won't. Phoebe, come on." He glances around, and his voice sounds even rougher than before. Desperate, maybe. His knuckles brush my arm through the fabric, and despite everything, I catch myself swaying closer. "Just stay a while longer."

"Why?" I try to sound cool, but it comes out so sour. "So I can make more drawings you hate?"

And I'm being such a baby, I know, but it only makes my temper flare higher. Why does this man's approval mean so freaking much to me? Knowing he doesn't like my artwork is the worst feeling in the world. I'm a pile of sludge in ripped jeans.

For the record, I don't care about most people's opinions,

and I take criticism from my drawing groups just fine. But with Sarge...

I guess after yesterday, I went all giddy over him.

"I don't hate your drawings," Sarge says, gripping the handle of my backpack like I might dash for the door. "Even a thug like me can see how talented you are, Phoebe."

"You're not a thug." A headache squeezes my skull, but I force a smile onto my face. I'm getting this all so wrong. And Sarge doesn't return my smile, scowling at me with those electric blue eyes. His coppery hair's all rumpled from the fight, and his cheeks are ruddy from the heat and exercise.

He really is a work of art. And he doesn't deserve my moods.

Come on, come on. Need to get out of here before I make this way worse.

"I've got everything I needed, thank you. This was really helpful." I'm saying all the right things, but Sarge still hasn't let go of my bag. He shifts closer where he's sitting on the mats, and with me standing, our faces are about level. I could grip his shoulders from here. I could sway forward until his breath tickles my cheeks. "I'll send you a copy of the finished art once it's done, if you like."

"Bring it to me in person," he orders. Is that how he got that name? By bossing people around? Or was he really a sergeant once?

"I live across town."

Sarge nods. "Then I'll come to you."

I huff, all flustered and crabby, and say the first thing that comes into my head. "Well, maybe I don't want you to know where I live."

And I'm just arguing for the sake of it, being a little toad, but I regret the words as soon as they leave my mouth.

Because Sarge's face shutters. He leans away and lets go of my bag.

"Of course."

The mats creak as he stands up, suddenly looming over me, but there's nothing threatening about him. Behind his eyes, he's far, far away.

"See you around, Phoebe."

I watch him walk away, and I'm hot and sick and miserable. Why did I say that? Why can't I be normal with people? Why am I like this?

You know, sometimes I wish I could be anyone else but me.

144

Sarge

✦✦✦

ere's what you need to know about this city's bare-knuckle circuit: it's secretive and lawless.

Fights take place in dockside warehouses; in abandoned train stations; on skyscraper rooftops. The prize money is steep and the bets are sky high. People gamble thousands on the outcome of each match, a river of money coursing through the bare-knuckle network, in and out of powerful pockets.

It's not what I dreamed of doing as a lad, but it more than pays the bills, and at least this way I can finish a goddamn fight. The half-done matches at The Corner are going to give me an ulcer.

Even here, I never cross a line. Never hurt my opponents in a way that won't heal—even though some, given the chance, would not return the favor.

We've all got to protect our own souls out here, because no one else will do it for us.

Tonight's match is on some billionaire's rooftop helipad, the space lent in return for making him feel alive. Stars dust the night sky high above, faded by the bright wash of floodlights, and crowds mill around, drinking and smoking and yelling like half of 'em aren't wearing designer suits.

I'm up last, slated to go against a Swedish fighter called Lars: blond and ham-fisted and wider than a park bench. Him and me, we've fought before. I knocked his tooth out, and he dislocated my shoulder.

Yeah, Lars is alright. We get on.

And as I swing my arms on the sidelines, waiting for the signal to step onto the floodlit helipad, I bite back a bitter smile.

I really need this.

Because it's been a week. A whole fucking week since Phoebe drew me at The Corner; a week since I ruffled up her blackbird feathers and put her off me for good.

Why'd I pick on her drawings like that? They were nice. Great, even, and I got so frazzled by the fact that she drew me like *that*, with her admiration clear in every pencil stroke, that I forgot to be a human about it.

No wonder she went all scrunchy and high-tailed it out of there like she couldn't get away fast enough. No wonder she didn't want me to know her address.

My gut hollows at the memory, those words still sickening me from the inside. *Maybe I don't want you to know where I live.*

Well, she's right. Why should a young woman like Phoebe trust an old brute like me? What gives me the right to expect that at all? I should've shrugged off her rejection, then coaxed her to stay a while and draw for me again, right there where she felt safe with me.

Should've done a lot of things. I roll my neck, wincing at the loud crack.

I'm stiff. Haven't been sleeping well lately.

"John Sergeant and Lars Larsson!" a voice booms, vibrating through pillars of black speakers. The crowd whoops and whistles, stamping their feet, and the night is cool as I step into the pool of light.

As soon as I move forward, all the sounds around me fade away. The screams; the stamping; the shriek of static crackling through the speakers. The wind whipping over the rooftop. Nothing registers except the calm thud of my heartbeat in my ears, and the slow drag of breath in and out of my lungs.

Lars is bare-chested like me, bouncing on his toes. He's broader but I'm taller with longer limbs; he's younger but I'm faster. We're well matched.

He nods, chin dipping, and I return the gesture. Respect is important. Else why are we both here?

A bell rings, the shrill sound drifting through my haze, and we both explode into motion, his shoulder slamming into my gut. I rain blows down on his bare back, teeth gritted, heels digging in as he shoves me back, and it's rough and brutal and wild.

Listen. I'm not saying this is nice. Not saying that bare-knuckle fighting is noble in any way. But I *am* saying that sometimes, this is the only way I feel at home in my body. And I'm built for it, might as well have been designed in a lab, because barely thirty seconds have passed and already Lars is buckling under my onslaught.

I shove him back; spit blood on the deck. Pursue him across the helipad to the roars of the crowd. What would Phoebe think of this?

I shake the thought off as soon as it comes. Can't afford the distraction.

This is going well. We're moving in tandem, the two of us caught up in a lethal dance, and Lars' eyes glitter with excitement too. Sometimes, when I'm really in the zone, I don't feel blows land on my body. I might hear the crunch of knuckles, might feel the force knocking me sideways, but there's no hot bloom of pain. That comes later.

The crowd is a blur. There's the gleam of white, perfectly straight teeth; the flash of a heavy wristwatch. Raised drinks, bubbles fizzing against the glass. And there—

Choppy black bangs and a bloodthirsty little smile. My heart stops, and Lars' punch hits me hard enough to make my head spin.

Staggering back, I raise my fists, but peer into the crowd. Was that her? Is Phoebe really here? Did she come for me?

Another blow snaps my head back, and the crowd groans as I stagger.

"Come on!" Lars yells, thumping my shoulder. "Focus, old man!"

Shit. Yeah. The fight snaps back into high definition, and I push all thoughts of doe eyes from my mind. Maybe she's here or maybe I hallucinated her, but either way, I don't want Phoebe to see me lose because I can't focus. Not even if she's a figment of my imagination. It's too humiliating.

Smack.

I land a solid punch, and Lars grins at me with bloodied teeth. We're back on, and the crowd howls its approval.

The whole fight lasts less than seven minutes. For us on the helipad, it's an eternity. But I'm not bored, and losing myself to this process is a kind of bliss, especially when in the back of my brain, I know Phoebe might be near.

I finish things quickly. No need to cause more harm than necessary, and with my knee in the center of Lars' back, the younger man spreadeagled on the floor, I wave one arm as the bell rings out my victory.

Suits are torn, glasses smashed, and already someone's turning up the music. Making this into a party. Well, I hope they'll all have a good night, but I've got someone to find.

Lars takes my offered hand, groaning as I pull him upright. "Good match," he mutters, spitting blood.

"You could've had me," I point out. "I let my mind wander like a prick."

Lars shrugs. "I don't want that kind of win."

Yeah, he's a good kid. We're cut from the same cloth, and I'm weirdly fond as I smack him on the shoulder. "Go get yourself a drink. They'll be cracking bottles worth more than your apartment, and I'm not even kidding."

His laugh is strained, but Lars staggers off in search of a fine whiskey, in nothing but black shorts. Good. He's earned it.

I drag my own t-shirt and sweatpants on over my shorts, peering around me as I shove my feet into my sneakers. This rooftop is huge, with the helipad only taking up one corner. There are gardens, too, and a swimming pool with loungers, and it's all rammed with people drinking and partying hard. I scan the crowd as best I can, moving stiffly as my injuries finally register, but I can't see Phoebe.

There's no evil little smile; no baggy plaid shirt. Did I dream her?

A finger prods my lower back. Relief courses through me, cool and sweet as a mountain breeze, and I turn slowly. Phoebe blinks up at me, mouth twisted. Her bangs are ruffled by the wind.

"You carry that thing everywhere, huh?"

She shrugs, the bag rocking on her back. "It's got my art stuff. I like being ready to draw."

"Makes sense." People push past us, flowing around us like two rocks in a river. Well—one big rock, and one cute little pebble. I was the main attraction just minutes ago, but now I'm old news, because bare knuckle crowds are like that. Fickle. But Phoebe's not looking away, and that warms my aching insides. "Listen, about before—"

"I'm sorry," she blurts, before I can go any further. She tugs a folded piece of paper from her plaid shirt pocket, handing it up to me. Her cheeks are flushed. "I made you this."

As I unfold the paper, my heart's jammed in my throat. There's a cartoon drawn in thick black pen: a little toad with choppy black hair and shit kicker boots on its feet. The toad looks sad, and there's a speech bubble which says, "Sorry."

Below the drawing, there's an address—right down to the apartment number. I swallow hard.

"You don't need to give me this."

"Yes, I do." Phoebe shrugs. "I want to. Now you can visit me."

"I can, huh?"

"Yeah."

Her boots scuff against the rooftop as she kicks her feet. She's fidgeting with nerves, as though I might tear up her gift and throw it to the stars.

As if. I'm gonna frame it and put it on my wall when I get home.

"Although I work shifts at the art supply store, and sometimes I go out drawing for hours. So you should text first." Phoebe jabs the paper in my hand. "I wrote down my number too."

"So I see." It's already committed to memory, burned into

150

my brain. Another gift I don't deserve; another show of trust. "Does this mean you've forgiven me?"

Her eyebrows shoot up, disappearing behind her bangs. "Have I forgiven you? What did *you* do wrong?"

I freaked her out. Forgot to tell her how good her drawings were. Generally messed things up, so I shrug. "I scared you off."

"Never," Phoebe mumbles, shaking her head, and hope swells so big inside me that if I'm not careful, I might crack a rib. In fact…

I rub my battered left side, wincing as I probe between the bones. There's some swelling, and it's growing. Worst timing ever, but that figures.

"I need to deal with…" I wave a bleeding hand at my whole body. "All of this." An idea nudges my brain, and there's no chance she'll go for it, but I ask anyway. It's that kind of night, because winning a fight can make a man feel invincible. "Want to come with?"

And miracle that she is, Phoebe grins. "Okay."

As I limp past her on the rooftop, she turns and slips her hand into mine.

Phoebe

There's a medic on the rooftop with a fold-out metal table, waving for Sarge to go and get checked over, but he ignores her and leads me through the crowd to the rooftop exit. In the elevator, he leans against the wall in pained silence.

It's a fancy elevator with mirrored walls and good lighting. It's vain, but I check myself out quickly, wincing at my rumpled hair and the bags under my eyes.

Haven't been sleeping well since I messed things up with Sarge. But we're okay now, right? So hopefully I'll sleep like a kitten tonight.

Besides, I may look tired and stressed, but Sarge literally just got his ass kicked. Oh, he won the fight and all, but not without taking his share of punches, and now the huge man looks kinda dizzy as he leans against the wall. There's a cut beneath his left eye, and his knuckles are swollen and bloody.

Sarge tilts his head, eyes slipping closed, and his breath fogs the mirror. I tug on his hand. "Should I go get that medic?"

The floor numbers flicker down, the elevator plunging silently through the building. Sarge draws in a ragged breath, then says, "Nope. I'm good." He cracks one eyelid. "I've got my own private nurse now, right?"

My cheeks warm, but I scowl at him. "I am not a trained medical professional."

"No?" The eyelid closes again. "Pity."

Ugh. Does he need the medic or not? Where are we even going?

"The Corner," he tells me in a tired voice when I ask. "I keep a full first aid kit there, and a bed if I need to crash after a fight. Means someone will definitely check on me in the morning, and make sure I'm not in too bad of a state."

That's... sad.

My chest pinches, and I squeeze his huge hand. *I* could check on him at his apartment if he wanted. You know, if he'd rather recover there. I'd happily do that for him.

Outside, we hail a cab easily and pass the ride in tense silence. At least, I'm tense. Sarge seems criminally relaxed, his head tipped back against the seat as his chest rises and falls, steady and slow. A thousand babyish thoughts batter my brain—like *why won't he talk to me*, and *it's like he doesn't want me here at all*—but I push them away.

I gave into my knee-jerk fears before, and look where that got us. The least I can do is give this man the benefit of the doubt, and remember that he just had a grueling fight, for god's sake. Of course he needs a minute.

"You okay over there?" Sarge's voice rumbles through the quiet cab. When I look over, his blue eyes are open, staring at me, their irises silvery in the moonlight.

I bite my lip and nod. "I'm good. Just wrestling with my

stupid brain, you know?"

"Ah." Sarge nods, the lines around his eyes softening. "Those can feel like fights to the death sometimes."

Tell me about it. "It's a real grudge match."

Sarge chuckles. Outside the cab windows, traffic sails past and neon lights throb. It's dark and cool and crowded out there, and I'm suddenly so grateful for these stolen minutes of quiet together.

If we were still on that rooftop, there would be howling crowds everywhere. People drinking and pushing, maybe trying to talk to Sarge. This way, it's just *us*. Alone in the velvet silence.

The cab's engine purrs quietly, and I can hear the steady thump of my heartbeat. It's faster than usual. Has been since I laid eyes on Sarge again.

Does he still like me? Back at The Corner, before I ruined everything, he seemed drawn to me too. We kept leaning into each other's space; kept shuffling closer, until our arms pressed together. Does he still want to touch me? Would he let me touch him?

The cab jolts over a pothole, and Sarge groans quietly. Maybe not tonight, then.

But maybe another night.

* * *

"Sit there." If I'm playing nurse, I'm gonna be one of those bossy matrons who rules over the ward with an iron fist. A freshly showered Sarge leans against the table with an amused huff.

We're in a room next to the gym's office. As promised, there's a full first aid kit, which I've spread over the windowsill; a table and lamp; an unmade camp bed with a pillow and folded sheets in the corner.

The lamp gives off a warm glow. Maybe I should put the overhead light on instead, but just the thought of it makes my temples ache.

Sarge has woken up a little since his shower. He's moving better too, less stiff and pained. It's like he powered down in that cab and woke up mostly recovered.

"Um." I pick up a bottle of antiseptic cream and squint at the label. "Maybe you should take your shirt off."

"For medical reasons?" Sarge teases, and yeah, he's feeling way better. His muscles bunch as he tugs the navy t-shirt over his head, baring his broad chest, the skin marred with grazes.

"Yeah. Let's say that's why."

We're flirting. *Flirting.* I've never flirted with a man in my whole freaking life. I've barely had a full platonic conversation, for that matter.

People just don't like me. I'm awkward and weird looking and I say the wrong things. But leaning against his table, Sarge stares like he wants to swallow me whole. Like he's a damp-haired tiger waiting to pounce.

"I guess I'll clean your cuts and grazes?" I hold up a pack of antiseptic wipes. "Is that right?"

He shrugs, and I've never seen him grin before, but it transforms his whole face. Those blue eyes crinkle, and his cheeks lift, and he looks five years younger. "If you say so."

"*Sarge.* What do you usually do after a fight? How do I take care of you?"

He sighs, but he's still smiling when he jerks his chin at the kit. "We'll need that second cream by your hip—yeah, that one—and those dressings. Ready to play nurse?"

Please. "I was born ready," I tell him, crossing to the table with my hands full of supplies. But even with him coaching me through each step, even with his patient instructions, I am not good at this.

"Whoops," I say, as the second dressing I've dropped flutters to the floor. My anxiety spikes, tightening my chest. "Sorry. Wait, just—stay there. Don't move. I'll get another one."

"Okay."

Sarge waits so patiently, and that makes it worse somehow. If he were alone, he'd probably be snoring on that camp bed by now.

"I suck at this."

"No, you don't." He nudges my hip with his knee. "You're doing just fine. There was a medic on that rooftop, remember? If anything goes wrong, it's my fault, not yours."

Wait, things could go wrong? Like what? How badly wrong? Is he in danger? The air suddenly feels thin, and band aid wrappers crinkle in my hands.

"Breathe," Sarge orders, and even though he's the injured one, I find my forehead resting on his shoulder. My hands grip his leg as he counts breaths for me, in and out. When did I get so panicky all the time? No wonder I've been hiding from the world. "You want me to take over, Phoebe?"

Yes. No.

"Is there much left?" I ask his collarbone.

"Nearly done," he says.

"Then no."

His hand cups the nape of my neck, his thumb rubbing the worst of my tension away. "You're a brave girl, Phoebe."

"For giving you shitty first aid?"

"For coming here alone with me. I appreciate the trust, sweet

156

girl."

There's no trust required. Or there is, I guess, but it's as easy as breathing once you get to know Sarge. Despite those bloody knuckles, he's a gentle giant. I had zero doubts, and I tell him so.

He hums, so pleased, and rests his chin on my head. I don't want to move away, and from the way he cups my neck, I don't think he wants me to move either.

If this were a page in my graphic novel, I'd draw just the one picture of us here, leaning against each other so peacefully. Then snowy white space on the rest of the page, to show how the rest of the world is far, far away, not intruding on this perfect moment. It's just us, and our shared breaths, and the warmth between our bodies.

Heaven.

"You ready to finish this up, nurse?" Sarge says after an age.

I grunt and straighten up, my joints creaking like I'm the fighter, not him. Enough daydreaming.

It's go time.

Sarge

Over the next month, we fall into a pattern. Phoebe draws me at The Corner most nights, and she comes to watch all my bare knuckle fights. Her savage little smile is my new good luck charm—the sight I scan for with each roaring crowd.

Afterward, she comes back to The Corner with me and practices her first aid skills, her husky little voice giving me a play by play of the fight, all while I close my battered eyes and savor the feeling of being alone with her.

Maybe it's wrong. Maybe I shouldn't make such a big deal of this, sucking up her presence like a plant absorbing sunlight. Maybe she's too young for me, and too spiky-sweet, and just a friend anyway.

I don't know. It's twisting up my insides each night, but I don't know.

Does she want me like I want her? Could I ever get that lucky?

She can't. It seems impossible, so I push the thought

away whenever it lingers in my mind. Whenever Phoebe leans against my side, her warmth spreading across my body; whenever her eyes linger on me, wide and beseeching, like she's trying to send me a silent message.

It's something else she wants from me. Company, maybe, or a big body to draw.

That's all.

* * *

This is another new habit: taking coffee to the art supply store where she works and helping her lock up at closing time. Phoebe scoffed the first time I suggested it, said I'd find it way too boring, but the truth is I'd cheerfully watch paint dry if we did it together. And I was looking for an excuse, any excuse to spend time with her—and luckily, she agreed.

Phoebe gets coffee, and I get to be near her for an hour or so. Win-win.

The bell jingles on the door as I push inside, a cardboard tray of two coffees held in one hand. The store's empty already, the sky darkening outside, and the air in here smells like paint and turpentine.

"Phoebe?"

"In here," she calls, her voice drifting from the stock cupboard behind the cash register.

I wander through the maze of art supplies: glossy sketch-books piled high on display tables, their snowy white pages completely untouched; lumps of charcoal in little dishes; racks of paints with wrinkly tester tubes. The smell gets stronger the deeper into the store I go.

Soft noises drift from the open stock cupboard door. The

rustle of cardboard sliding together; the creak of floorboards; the sound of Phoebe cursing under her breath. It's just as well that she doesn't work in a kid's store, because my girl swears like a sailor when she's lost in her task.

"Coffee," I call, placing the tray on the table beside the cash register. Spots of rain from the walk here dot the white lids, and I brush my damp shoulders, suddenly self conscious. Do I smell musty?

"Thank freaking god." Phoebe bursts out of the stock cupboard, red-cheeked and frazzled, smacking her dusty hands together. Her bangs are all rumpled, and the name tag she wears for work is twisted up in her red t-shirt. It says: *Hi, my name is Wendy!*

"This has been the longest hour of my life," she says, snatching up her coffee cup.

"I'm sorry to hear that, Wendy."

The glare she sends me over the top of her drink could incinerate a man at twenty paces. Worth it.

"Should I lock the front door?"

Phoebe grunts. That means yes. Over the last month, I've become fluent in Phoebe's surly noises and body language.

The walk back through the art supply maze gives me a chance to sniff my gray shirt and check for underarm stains. Not perfect but it'll do. I rake my fingers through my damp hair, too, and give myself a mini pep talk.

She likes the coffee I bring her. It's okay that I'm here.

She'd tell me to leave if she wanted to.

When I reach the door, I hold it open for a few seconds first, breathing in the rain-fresh air from the street. Letting the cool breeze soothe my ruddy cheeks. Then I close it and spin the lock with a soft click, and try not to think about how alone we are.

Dark shapes move past the windows, hurrying through the spitting rain outside. People walking home from work, or out to meet friends. People going about their lives, headlights from cars shining between their bodies, and meanwhile Phoebe and I are here in this quiet, empty shop. In our bubble.

She's perched on the stool behind the cash register when I rejoin her, sucking down her coffee like it's the elixir of life. Clutching the cup with both hands, her throat moving as she swallows, her eyes closed with bliss.

This is why I bring her coffees at the end of her shift. I'd bring them at the start and on her lunch break too, if that wouldn't make me look unhinged.

I flick her knee when I reach her, right on a patch of bare skin. It's easy to do when she wears those ripped jeans.

A combat boot swings out, kicking gently at my leg. She's still drinking, eyes closed.

"Should I leave the two of you alone?"

Phoebe makes a small noise and shakes her head. She tips the cup higher, still drinking. Has she breathed in the last minute? Does this woman have gills?

My girl drains the last drop before placing the empty container down. A tiny burp escapes before she claps a hand over her mouth, and she blinks up at me, horrified.

I smirk down at her, peeling the lid off my own untouched coffee. "Such a little beast, Phoebe. I should donate you to a petting zoo."

"Shut up," she whispers, but when she drops her hands, her cheeks are bright red. Then, louder: "I didn't expect you today. Figured you'd be getting ready for tonight's fight."

I shrug, but I can't meet her eye. "I am getting ready."

"By drinking a caramel latte?"

Damn. Should never have told her my order. "By spending time with you. It helps me relax."

And it's true, all true, but as soon as the words are out, I wish I could snatch them back, because that confession is too raw, too intimate. Too much pressure. What if I scare her away?

"Oh," Phoebe says, and silence thickens between us.

Shit. Fuck. Shit.

"I didn't mean that," I blurt, right as she says: "Really?" Hope flickers across her face, then immediately dies. She goes to drink from her cup, then remembers it's empty.

Silence again, but with an undercurrent of hurt this time. Jesus Christ, put me out of my misery here. Peering up at the cobwebbed store ceiling, I pray for a lightning bolt. A sudden sinkhole opening beneath me. Anything.

This is why I've never got close to anyone before; why I've always been alone. Any chance I get, I cram my whole foot in my mouth. And it's been lonely, sure, but it never truly bothered me until I met Phoebe.

Now every blunder I make bruises my insides.

She puffs out a tiny sigh and talks to her knees. "You know, I wish you did mean it, Sarge."

I clear my throat, and it sounds like rocks shifting. "What's that?"

"I wish spending time with me helped you relax. No one relaxes around me, you know? I set people on edge; make them uncomfortable. I'm weird."

Hell no. "You're not weird. You're perfect."

"I *am* weird, but if you like me..." She glances up, finally. Fixes me with those big, brown eyes. "Then I don't mind so much."

Ah, Christ. Look at us.

We're two lonely peas in a pod.

"I do like you," I tell her, my voice rough. Why haven't I made it clearer? If I'm not telling her this stuff every day, then what am I even good for? "Of course I like you. When you're not around, I'm fucking miserable, Phoebe."

She sits a little straighter, her shoulders dropping back in her red shirt. "Really?" Then, quickly: "Don't take it back this time. Not if you mean it."

"I mean it." Of course I do. "If it was a choice between every other fucker in the universe or you, I'd choose you. Every time, Phoebe."

"Oh," she says again. "In that case."

When she slides off the stool, dropping to her knees, it takes me a shameful amount of time to realize what she's planning.

Slender fingers find my pants button. They flick it open, then tug down the zip.

"Christ," I mutter at last, my big hands flailing. One lands on the table, gripping the edge so hard the wood creaks, and the other buries into Phoebe's dark, silky hair. And I can't believe she's down there—can't believe I'm allowed to touch her hair—

"Is this okay?" Phoebe asks softly, stroking both palms up my tensed thighs. She's got my pants open now, but she's not gone in there at all. "Sarge. Are you having a stroke up there?"

"Yeah." Christ. Yes to both. "It's okay. But you don't have to do this, Phoebe, I would never expect—"

She scoffs, cutting me off. "*I* know that." Shifting her weight, she settles more firmly on her knees. "But I've thought about this before."

She has? "You have?"

"Lots of times. I've, um. I've drawn it, actually. What we

might be like together. You and me." Her cheeks are pink, getting pinker, and she's so small down there. "Sucking your cock. Having—having sex. I think we'd look good. I think we'd *feel* good."

God above, my ears are ringing. I sift through her hair with one hand, letting the touch anchor me, and I'd give my life savings for one of those drawings.

But when Phoebe leans forward, I hold her back with a gentle tug on her hair.

One more thing. One more question, before the last ounce of my self control is gone.

"This isn't just sex, right?" My voice is ragged, and she hasn't even touched me yet. Not beyond the soothing stroke up and down my thighs. "I can't just—Phoebe, I can't just mess around. That's not the man I am. If you start this with me, if you do this, I'll want everything. You understand?"

"Everything?" Her smile is mischievous, and she rests her pointy chin on my thigh. Gazes up at me with sparkling eyes. "Do you promise?"

Okay, that's it. Asked and answered.

I grip her hair harder, and guide her mouth toward my bulge. "Yeah, I promise. Now touch me, you little tease."

Phoebe

I *'ll want everything.* Sarge's warning pounds through my bloodstream as I slide one hand into his pants, his deep growl echoing in my brain. He said it like he was breaking terrible news, and not offering me a winning lottery ticket. Jeez, does this man not realize by now how badly I want him?

Time to show him, since words don't work. Far above me, Sarge grunts as my fingertips brush his hot skin between the folds of fabric.

He's long and thick and ruddy, a vein pulsing in his shaft as I draw it into the cool air. His cock is heavy against my palm, and so big my fingers can't wrap all the way around it. My eyes widen, and I can't help shooting a startled glance to the man standing over me.

"Sorry." He's rueful. "I'm a big man all over."

Tell me about it. Kneeling down here at his feet, his huge body looming so high above that my neck aches when I meet his eye—it makes me feel so delicate and tiny.

Like he could squish me like a bug. Or, no—like he could put me in his pocket, or carry me around on the palm of his hand. Taking care of me like his pretty little pet.

I bite my lip, giving his shaft an experimental stroke. Sarge groans, shoulders curving in like I've punched him in the gut, and... wow.

This feels powerful.

He's a bare knuckle champion, a man who could tear apart a brick wall with his bare hands, and he's grunting with every stroke of my fingers. Breathing hard like I've got him on the ropes.

He's at my mercy, and the vicious little imp inside of me loves that. But this is *Sarge*, so even if I hold all the power in this moment, I want to use that power for good.

The floorboards creak as I lean forward and press a kiss against the tip. It's close-lipped and chaste, a bead of salty fluid spreading over my lips, but Sarge hisses like I've pulled out some crazy move. A suspicion tickles my brain.

"Have you done this before?" My voice floats through the quiet, and my tongue lashes out right after, flicking over the ruddy head. Sarge shifts his feet and shakes his head.

"None of it," he rasps, and the way his cheeks flush and shoulders climb, he seems... embarrassed. And nope. No, that's not okay.

When I squeeze his cock, it jumps against my palm. Does he seriously think I'd prefer him all experienced? This way he's *mine*, all mine in the most primal way. "Good. Me neither. We can figure it all out together."

"Yeah?" Sarge breathes harder now, his grip firmer in my hair as he guides my mouth back where he wants it. Slowly, his shoulders drop away from his ears. And I open up, obedient for the first time in my freaking life, to suck the bulbous head

166

past my lips.

It's salty and warm, so heavy on my tongue. So soothing.

I hum happily, my hands trailing over his thighs, his shaft, his hips. Slipping under his t-shirt to rub at the furry line tracking down his firm belly. Sarge is stronger than an ox, but there's no six pack here, and I love how *real* he is.

"Christ," he mutters as I bob my head, setting a rhythm. "Phoebe, the way you feel—"

He breaks off, glancing out toward the street, cheeks even darker now. And how would this look, if someone peered through the foggy store windows? I'm hidden by the table, kneeling between Sarge's big feet, but he's just standing up there, facing the wall. Talking to the empty air.

I snort, eyes watering, and my giggles vibrate through his silky skin. Sarge shakes his head, working my mouth over him via the strong grip on my hair, and it's so merciless the way he holds me there, ragged breaths coming through my nose. I love it.

"Not going to ask, Phoebe. Not going to think about why you're eye to eye with my cock and having a laughing fit. Call it denial, but I'm not even going to go there."

I snort again, gripping his thighs for balance, and he chuckles too. Spreads his feet wider, the floor groaning under his weight, then pushes me harder against his cock.

And I love that he's gone all stern, taking control. Love being bossed around and directed and moved into position. Love being a warm mouth he can claim, his shaft plunging in and out and stroking over my pliant tongue, my eyes watering as he knocks against the back of my throat.

My gentle giant.

Mine.

A slideshow of things he could do to me flickers through my brain. Sarge holding me down and spreading me open, his fingertips bruising my thighs; Sarge mounting me from behind, one meaty hand wrapped over my mouth, gagging me; being taken and used and overcome. My whole body flushes hot, my pulse pounding between my legs, and I squirm against the floor, trying to jam my heel somewhere I can rub against it.

"Breathe," Sarge orders, pulling my mouth away with a pop. I slump to one side, wheezing and smiling up at him, so dazed and happy, and I could spend the rest of my life on my knees for this man. "You okay down there?" Worry flickers across his blue eyes. "Phoebe? You want to stop?"

"No," I croak. "I don't want to stop. I never want to stop."

Sarge's relieved smile is like the sun coming out. "Me neither, sweet girl. Christ, you're so perfect."

I don't feel perfect, not with my eyes watering and drool on my chin, my red t-shirt sticking to my back with sweat. But the way Sarge stares down at me, you'd think I'm ready for a magazine spread.

I lean forward again, tongue flicking over my bottom lip, but Sarge holds me back by my hair. I mewl, frustrated, but he ignores me.

"Do you... Phoebe, do you want to do more? Right now?" He gusts out a sigh, a blunt thumb rubbing at the base of my skull. "Because I can't do both. With the way your mouth feels, I won't last that way much longer."

Um, hell yes I want to do more, and I want to wipe away the shame creeping over Sarge's face too. Who cares if we don't set any records tonight? It's our first time, damn it. There's no one to impress but ourselves.

"Yeah, I do. Maybe... maybe if you sit here? And lean against the wall? So you're hidden from the street?"

We fumble around, knocking into the cash register, our hushed laughs drifting through the store.

You don't get these panels in the naughtier comic books I've read. You know: the logistics. It's all high-points only, with artfully arranged limbs. Screaming climaxes and arched spines.

This is better, though. For starters, if I only got the edited highlights, I'd miss Sarge thumping and cursing his way onto the floor, pants open and shirt rucked. To be fair to him, it's a long way to travel. Like a redwood being felled.

And when I stand on wobbly legs, kicking off my boots and socks and shoving down my ripped jeans and underwear—I'm no better. There is zero grace right now in this store. We're both too eager and worked up, both half-expecting someone to leap out and yell: *Surprise! You don't really get to be this happy!*

"Ready?" I bound into his lap, landing in a sprawl of flushed limbs. He barks out a laugh, holding me up by the waist even though his cock is right there, so close and hard and shiny with my spit.

"Phoebe." The head nudges against my inner thigh, smearing a sticky trail, and I pant and squirm, trying to get closer. *"Phoebe. Jesus Christ, you've gone feral."*

My cheeks ache from grinning, and I love this. Love wrestling with this mountain of a man, trying to fight my way onto his cock. Love the pained way he laughs, like he'd love nothing better than to let me win.

"I need to get you ready for me. Phoebe! You need my fingers or my tongue first."

What I need is his giant cock to split me open. Duh.

But a few minutes with his mouth between my legs changes my tune. This is the best thing I've ever felt, so hot and slick and tingly. Every time his stubble scrapes my thighs, I melt.

Sarge groans, pressing his face closer; plunges his tongue all the way inside me. His eyes are half-lidded. He looks lost to this: to my taste, my clenching body. Like he could do this for hours and hours and never let up.

"Enough," I mumble at last, batting at his shoulder. He finally leans back, breathing hard, and his mouth is shiny, his lips redder than before. Those blues eyes are nearly swallowed up with black. "I need to feel you. Please?"

There's a stunned beat, then Sarge shakes his head. Laughs softly, lowering me back down into his lap. "This isn't real, Phoebe. This is a dream. Ouch—hey!"

"You're supposed to pinch yourself if you're not sure. Everyone knows that." Gripping his cock and guiding it between my thighs, I smirk at the fighter. "You'll get worse than that later at your match."

"I'll be expecting it at the match," he points out, but he's not even paying attention to our bickering. Not really. He's staring, laser focused, at where his shaft prods at the entrance to my body. "Phoebe. Are you sure?"

"So sure." Surer than I've ever been in my whole lonely life. Spreading my legs an inch more, I grip Sarge's massive shoulders—and sink down.

Sarge

〜∽∂⌒⌒∂∽〜

Tight. Christ, she's tight and hot and slick, strangling me in a death grip as I press into her body. I grunt, head thumping against the wall, and I'm holding her hips too tight, thrusting up when I shouldn't yet, but it's so *much.*

Can't think. Can't fucking think.

"Oh," Phoebe breathes, and that flush on her cheekbones is the best thing I've ever seen. She scrabbles at my chest, eyes fluttering closed as she sinks down another few inches. "Oh. Oh my god."

"Doing okay?" I grind out, and god help me, if my girl says no, I *will* stop.

Even if it takes every ounce of will power in my body; even if it feels like dying inside. We're not doing this unless it feels good for her too, and she's so damn small compared to me. So tiny and breakable.

"Phoebe? You okay?"

"S-so good." The words shiver out of her, and I melt back

171

against the wall, suddenly boneless for a few breaths. Thank god. "Sarge. You feel *so* good." An amused flicker across her face. "So this is why everyone screws around."

"You won't." The words punch out of me, low and rough, and I'm tense again, but Phoebe doesn't mind. She's not scared of me, never was. And she tilts her head, smiling dreamily like I'm reading her a sonnet and not laying down the law.

Can't help it. The thought of her doing this with anyone else—hell no.

"Don't care if you're curious." My hips thrust up beneath her, claiming another tight inch. My chest burns. "You're not riding any other cocks, Phoebe. You're *mine*, do you hear? Only mine."

"Only yours," she repeats softly, her smile so blissed out as she rises and falls over my lap. Her eyelids flutter open, and she fixes me with that soulful brown gaze. "Always, Sarge."

Always. Yeah. And I'm hers too, all hers; she can do whatever she wants with me. Can draw me and bed me and ride around on my goddamn shoulders.

Phoebe grinds herself against my lap, whimpering, and we're fully sealed now. I'm thrust all the way inside her, throbbing and fighting not to burst, and every time she moves over me, I see stars.

So good. So good.

I squeeze her hips and thrust deeper. Bite off a groan.

And when her slender fingers trace over my cheeks, when she tilts my head up to face her, I'm half gone already. Lost in the wild pleasure of her body.

Phoebe's dark hair swings forward, tickling my neck, and her breath puffs against my lips. "You haven't kissed me yet," she whispers.

I haven't? How can that be right? I sort through my memories, grunting as she rides me faster, grinds harder against my lap, but she's right. All the images I have of the two of us kissing are ones I dreamed up on sleepless nights.

Damn. Well, we're doing this all out of order, but we *are* doing it. Cupping the side of her throat, I tug her down.

Phoebe smiles against my mouth, lips curving.

And we're both flushed and breathless, salty with sweat. Both clumsy and eager. But as our mouths slant together, our bodies melting with relief, a final knot of tension unwinds in my gut.

We're here. Doing this.

It's real.

And once I've started kissing her, I can't stop. I kiss her, slow and filthy, as she rides my shaft; I swallow her whimpers as my thumb finds her clit. I kiss Phoebe until sounds fade and lights dim and there's nothing but the electric tingle of friction where our bodies meet. Nothing but my girl.

"Sarge," she begs.

"It's John," I tell her, so quiet only she can hear. No one's called me by my real name since I was a lad, exploding head and shoulders above everyone else in a legendary growth spurt. Turned from person to freak show. I want Phoebe to call me by my real name.

"John," she whispers, and I stiffen, swelling inside her. Throbbing with need.

My thumb aches as I swirl it over her clit, but I don't stop, not until she's shaking and moaning, her body clenching on my length.

I make extra damn sure that she's come, her cheeks burning hot and her eyes hazy. Then I shove myself as deep as I can go, burying to the hilt inside her—and I relax, all the troubles of the world melting into pure, primal bliss as I pump her full. Spurt after spurt of wet heat, and I thrust deeper. *Deeper.*

Then slump back against the wall breathing hard, and grin when Phoebe catches my eye. She raises a mischievous eyebrow.

"You'd better win that fight tonight, John Sergeant. No excuses, just 'cause I screwed your brains out."

My laugh echoes through the empty store.

Finally.

She's mine.

* * *

Two years later

The Corner's lights shine extra bright overhead, lighting up the huge white room. The gym's busy, but no one's fighting in here. Not yet, anyway. The people in this crowd chat and mill around, sipping from flutes of champagne, and most of them have clearly never seen a fight in their lives.

They're artists and writers. Journalists and publishing staff, along with a few stray members of the public. When we suggested this venue for Phoebe's book launch, the marketing team was startled—then thrilled.

The famous boxing gym downtown? Owned by *the* Jax Sutherland? Would the two of us fight and lend some extra excitement?

Phoebe seemed embarrassed to ask me this favor, but I agreed before she finished the question. Anything I can do for my wife, I will.

"It's always the quiet crowds," Jax murmurs as he comes to

stand by my side. He jiggles his daughter on his hip, and she bursts into giggles, tugging at his t-shirt. When the fight starts, Casey will spirit their daughter away somewhere so she won't see me kick her daddy's ass. Fingers crossed, anyway. "They start the night all polite, but as soon as the bell rings, they'll be baying for blood."

I shrug. "If it launches Phoebe's book..."

Jax nods, quick to agree. "No kidding."

Besides, what could be more perfect than launching her graphic novel with a fight? I'm in those pages, after all. Maybe you wouldn't recognize me at first glance—the character Phoebe created with my features is dark haired instead, with a grizzled beard—but once we start fighting, it'll be clear.

"Can't believe she based her hero on you," Jax says, and when I look over, the jackass is stifling a grin. "You're more the villain build."

"Watch it." I wink at Jax's daughter, and she sticks her tongue out. Phoebe's bump is getting bigger by the day, and I wonder for the millionth time whether it will be a boy or a girl. A slender, mischievous thing or a future giant.

Time will tell. Christ, I can't wait.

"Hey, man." Dawson, another regular, thumps Jax's other shoulder, his wife Lara cuddling their toddler by his side. They joke together, laughing and teasing, but I let it all fade away. I'm too busy staring at the woman sitting at a nearby table, signing a stack of graphic novels for a line of readers.

Grabbing a copy from the nearest table, I get in line. Phoebe scoffs when she spots me a few spaces away, but she keeps going, signing her name with that spiky signature she likes. It suits her.

"We have so, so many copies at home." Phoebe rolls her eyes

when I place my new book in front of her, but she peels the glossy front cover open. "And who is this for?"

"Make it out to your beloved husband. No—the sire of your child. Wait, no, the love of your life. Or how about—"

"Done." Phoebe slaps the book shut and smirks at me. "Pay up, John Sergeant. And move your ass, because there's a line."

I grin at her, shark-like, and lean over to kiss her forehead before moving along. My feet turn to the boxing ring in the center of the room, and I flip the cover open idly as I walk.

I stop, my chest suddenly warm.

To my muse, she's written. Three words, and I'm cracked wide open in the middle of this brightly-lit gym, overcome with love and awe and so many goddamn feelings.

When I glance back, Phoebe's watching me. She smirks, one hand tracing over the swell of her belly.

Right. I march toward the boxing ring, yanking my t-shirt over my head. Time to make this crowd roar.

Anything for my bloodthirsty girl.

* * *

Thanks for reading the Blood, Sweat & Kisses series! I hope you loved it. :)

For more gritty instalove in the city, check out the Sweet Little Sinners series. *It's a lawless city, filled with mobsters and rogues. But it's the girls you should watch out for.*

And for a bonus instalove story, grab your copy of Ride or Die. *She's sweet and innocent—and that's like catnip in this strip club. It's okay, though. I won't let the pretty bartender out of my sight.*

Happy reading!

xxx

Teaser: Thief

❧

I flop out of the suitcase onto hardwood floorboards, cheeks hot and breathing hard. It was *cramped* in there. Hot and dark and stifling. If I'd waited one more hour, my muscles would've locked.

There are more comfortable ways to break into an apartment, that's for sure. Picking locks or squeezing through windows. Wriggling through air conditioning shafts. But being carried in, zipped away in luggage or taped in a cardboard box—that's my favorite. They might as well roll out the welcome mat. So pleasing.

My joints pop as I stretch out my limbs, reveling in all this sudden space and fresh air. Spencer Arnoult's penthouse is dark, all silence and shadows, but even in the gloom I can tell this place is *nice*. Laying back on the hallway floorboards, I count four big paintings on the walls and a small sculpture of a cresting wave on a plinth.

Not what you'd expect from a tech bro, I'll give him that. I'd pictured purple neon floor lights and cheeto-dust fingerprints on everything. Framed posters of naked women and tentacle monsters. Instead, the apartment smells like orange blossom and night air, and the furnishings I can make out are downright tasteful.

So the guy's mature and artsy. I like that. There's nothing more depressing than a rich man's apartment filled with chrome and glass and nothing else—all white walls and sharp edges and zero personality. An airport lounge made chic.

I mean, I should know. I burgle enough of them.

Resting one palm on my stomach, I focus on slowing down my gasping breaths. Getting calm. Centered and ready. The most uncomfortable part of the night is over but my work has just begun, and the last thing I need is to be rushed and sloppy.

Somewhere in this penthouse is a priceless jewel. Spencer Arnoult bought it at auction last week, and in all his cocky glory, he didn't store it in a bank vault. He had it delivered *here*, to his apartment in the city. Practically dangled it under my nose.

And it's a beautiful jewel. A fist-sized sapphire the color of ocean mist. I'm going to find it, lick it, and keep it.

"C'mon, girl." I always time my little visits for when no one's home. It's safer, obviously, but it also means no one hears me talking to myself as I roll onto my side, stiff muscles aching, and push onto my hands and knees. This is part of the routine, too.

Cow pose.

Cat pose.

Downward facing dog.

If my burgling luck ever runs out, maybe I'll teach yoga in prison.

I'm still shaking out my stiff arms two minutes later, padding softly through Spencer Arnoult's kitchen. I never wear shoes to burgle. Can you imagine sharing that cramped suitcase with a pair of sneakers? Besides, shoes leave prints, and I don't leave clues behind. That's amateur hour. Black socks work just fine, along with black leggings, black gloves, a black long-sleeved top, and a black beanie to tuck away my long hair.

Hey, I like black. And it's kind of a uniform for burglars—not that there's anyone here to admire my outfit. I give a twirl anyway, even though it's just me and this marble-top kitchen island, this vintage wine rack, and this stainless steel refrigerator, my reflection spinning across the gleaming surface.

My steps pause.

My stomach growls.

Huh. I *am* pretty hungry. And burgling is hard work—it's non-stop adrenaline for days before and after.

Light spills across the kitchen tiles as I tug the refrigerator door open, peering in at Spencer Arnoult's shelves of food. God, I can never resist exploring when I break in somewhere, even when I'm on the clock. It's just so *delicious*, seeing behind the curtain like this. Sneaking behind enemy lines. It makes my insides go all tingly.

And you want to get to know a man? Take a look at his groceries. Here, one peek tells me that Spencer Arnoult has fine tastes, a healthy appetite, and probably cooks for himself. His shelves burst with fine cheeses and cured meats; pots of olives and fancy hummus. Ripe, colorful fruits and vegetables, rows of eggs, and glass bottles of milk.

Boring. But there's a carton of leftover takeout noodles tucked away at the back, and my flushed face melts into a smirk. *I* see you, Spencer Arnoult. Your veggies don't fool me. I reach past the healthy stuff and snag the takeout container, pulling it down for a sniff.

Satay chicken. Fresh, too. *Hell* yeah.

One quick search for the microwave later, my surprise dinner hums as it heats up, spinning in the golden light. I lean against the kitchen island, sipping a tall glass of water, feeling so pleased with myself I could purr. Is this evil? I feel kind of evil. Not about the sapphire—no one *needs* one of those—but about stealing his leftovers.

I know if anyone ever dared rob *me*, that's what would piss me off most, right before I returned the favor. Because I treasure my leftovers. I lust over my meals for hours beforehand, imagining each perfect bite. Food takes up constant real estate in my brain, and I don't mean to brag, but it's a pretty big brain.

Stealing these leftovers... I'm not proud of it. Not exactly. But Spencer Arnoult is not here, and since he left town without those precious noodles, he clearly doesn't love them like I do.

So food first.

And maybe I'll dig through his bedroom drawers. A girl's gotta know.

Then I'll find the jewel. Easy peasy.

* * *

It's always surreal being inside a celebrity's private space. Not that I make a habit of burgling famous actors or whatever—not unless they have something pretty I really want—but wealthy people have their own orbit. It's impossible *not* to be aware of them, at least on some level.

And Spencer Arnoult has been in plenty of headlines over the last few years. He's been plastered over the twenty-four news cycle along with all those other Silicon Valley boy wonders, and though he left those roots behind when he came to this city in his mid-thirties, trading in his zip up hoodies for button-down shirts, his bank balance and billion dollar company came with him.

So I've seen his face plenty of times; I've heard his deep, stilted voice in interviews. I know *of* him. The man, the myth, the legend. That square jaw and the thick framed glasses. A stammering, pin-up Clark Kent.

And now I'm slurping his chicken satay noodles and sitting cross-legged on his couch, wriggling my sore ass against the cushions. His couch is forest green, covered in soft but sturdy fabric and draped with a fleecy cream throw.

It's kind of trashy, and I love it. He's got shockingly enjoyable taste. Sometimes I break into these penthouses and mansions, and there's so little personality I just want to scream at the off-white walls.

This place, though? It's homey. Fun yet soothing. Those other richies could learn a thing or two from Spencer Arnoult–and maybe I'll have to burgle him again. Come back and see what he's changed around the place.

I bite my lip as I prod the noodles with my fork. Peanut-scented steam curls over my cheeks, and I fish out a lump of chicken breast. How long did Frankie say he's away on business for? Three whole days?

Maybe I could stay the weekend, playing house with the ghost of a billionaire. There's plenty of food in the fridge.

Ha. Lil' old me, in an apartment like this. Could you ever imagine?

* * *

Check out Thief in the Sweet Little Sinners collection!

182

Cassie Mint

About the Author

Cassie writes outrageous, OTT instalove with tons of sugar and spice. She loves cookie dough, summer barbecues, and her gorgeous cat Missy.

You can connect with me on:
- https://www.authorcassiemint.com
- https://www.facebook.com/cassiemintauthor
- https://www.bookbub.com/authors/cassie-mint

Subscribe to my newsletter:
- https://www.authorcassiemint.com/newsletter